THE GHOST IN ROOM 785

BONNIE ELIZABETH

My Big Fat Orange Cat Publishing

The Ghost in Room 785
My Big Fat Orange Cat
Mystery 2024

My Big Fat Orange Cat Publishing
MyBigFatOrangeCat.com

ISBN: 978-1-953363-25-1

Chapter One

I quite enjoy talking to the guests as they come into my hotel. My days are filled with living vicariously through other people's travels and the joy they take in seeing this part of Appalachia. The Neary-Ten is a huge hotel originally built over a hundred years ago with additions added as the times changed along with the guest's needs.

As hotel manager, it's my job to know what's going on and to answer questions. Some, like why is the hotel called The Neary-Ten—answer: because it's nearly to Tennessee and our owners thought it was a good name—I have answered over and over again. Others, like whether any of our restaurants served Vegemite were less common, particularly as the guest didn't sound Australian nor are we in any way shape or form advertised as having any sort of Australian theme.

The Neary-Ten is a haunted hotel and that is how I advertise it. I get a lot of guests who come to see the ghosts.

Jean Marshall, a charming woman, was there that afternoon in her tailored blue jeans and white knit tank top with little red bows around the neckline, asking about our ghosts. She told me, and my desk worker, Suzanne, all about how she always chose hotels based on whether or not they were haunted. Her short gray hair was trimmed perfectly and her look was more in tune with the guests who come to enjoy our spa than with our ghost hunters, not that I should judge.

We'd just finished chatting and I'd gotten one of our porters to assist her with her small designer carry-on and oversized tote when I looked up to see Floyd Bowman coming into the hotel. The Bowman family, as a collective, own the Neary-Ten. Floyd was the annoying middle brother who constantly tried to outshine his other siblings. He had an older brother and two older sisters as well as a younger brother and sister. Floyd was the only one who really seemed to think he knew about hotel management. I had not been able to convince him otherwise.

Normally, he's a thorn in my side on the phone or, nowadays, on Zoom calls. Today, he had come to the hotel without warning.

His stiff black suit jacket and slacks were out of place in the hotel. While our floors were white tile to brighten the place on dark winter days, the stone fireplace and the detailed woodwork around the windows that lined the front gave the hotel more of a mountain resort feel. He kept his eyes on Jean while she talked with the porter helping her over near the elevators. She had suite 785, which was supposed to be haunted, though I had yet to see a ghost there.

The lobby bar had been busy at lunch serving pizzas so the smell of garlic and pepperoni wafted out. I noticed Floyd wrinkling his nose. He'd probably tell me to find a way to vent the bar better so the smell didn't drift into the lobby. As if that were possible. Besides, people came here from around the area. It was no small trip for many of them, so it said something about how popular the bar was.

I slipped into my office, pretending not to have noticed him. If Suzanne knew why, she didn't say a word. While Floyd might give her a hard time, I doubted he'd be as rude to a regular worker as he would be to me. I was supposed to be in charge and anticipate his every whim. Besides, Suzanne had proven herself able to work with Olive, the ghost of our former, rather persnickety manager, on her book so I felt she was more than capable of handling Floyd.

The door to my office stayed open as the space was far too small to close the door on a regular basis. I had a couple of chairs, a huge desk and some built-in bookcases for storage. It always smelled of smoke no matter that I'd had the room repainted. I knew from Olive that before she'd died, she'd also had the office redone.

Yes, Olive is a ghost and she was once the manger of the hotel. She's also one of my closest friends, though I have to admit I have no desire to join her in managing the place in the afterlife. In fact, the very idea of it sometimes gave me the shudders.

The soft piano music I had in the background reached me in the office though there were no speakers. As it got later, the music from the lobby bar would turn up and the beat would get going a bit more. At least Floyd hadn't come in while that was happening. I knew he didn't like popular music and that's what the lobby bar always played. If he had his way, they'd only play classical jazz, which is nice, but that's the atmosphere in the upstairs mezzanine bar which is a little more contained.

"I'm sorry, we don't have a reservation," Suzanne told him.

I kept my head down as if I were studying something intently on my computer screen.

"I need to speak to Ms. Davenport," Floyd said. He spoke with something like an English accent though I knew he'd never lived over there. Given how much money the family had, I suspected he'd traveled to London but he was more anglophile than actual Brit. It was one of many things that irritated me about Floyd.

"Okay," Suzanne drew the word out.

While my eyes stayed on the computer screen, I noted the way her body turned as if to call me from my office. When I didn't look up, she walked over to me. The music was soft enough that I heard her shoes squeak on the floor as she stepped.

"Maggie?" Suzanne called.

I looked up as if surprised to see her, when in actuality I had been counting the seconds hoping to draw out the time.

"Yes?" As if I didn't know exactly what she needed. As if she didn't know I always overheard what went on at the desk, and, in most cases, I would have been standing up to help before Floyd had finished his request.

"There's someone here without a reservation. He wants the Royal Suite, but…"

But it was booked. We had a honeymoon couple up there right now and I wasn't about to move them.

I stood up and went to the desk.

"Hello, Mr. Bowman," I said. While the other siblings all preferred to be addressed by their first names, Floyd liked to be addressed as Mr. Bowman, rather as if he worried that if he didn't remind people he was a Bowman they might forget.

"Ms. Davenport," Floyd said. I did have to admit that while he was stupidly insistent upon being accorded formal respect, he did do the same to the rest of us, though I found it grating, rather as if I were going to be taken to task for something. Granted, Floyd usually found something to take me to task for, even if it was stupid, but all the same, he didn't have to start out that way in every conversation.

"I don't believe we had notice that you were going to be here," I said pleasantly. Had we done so, I'd have made sure he had the Royal Suite, which he preferred to the Owner's Suite. The Royal suite had a piano in the sitting area. The Owner's suite did not. Other than that, they were identical. Apparently, he'd been overruled when requesting a grand piano for both suites. The rest of the family knew they'd never use it, nor would he, so far as I knew.

"I need the Royal Suite please," he said.

"I'm very sorry but we have a honeymoon couple booked in there for two more days," I said. "We do have the Owner's Suite, if you'd like?"

"I would not," he said. "Move the couple."

"I can't just do that," I said. "The Royal Suite is a higher end suite than the Owner's Suite and they've paid good money for it. Her sister is planning her own wedding and is consulting with us about having it here so if the bride is unhappy, we stand to lose quite a bit of business, not to mention a poor rating online."

Floyd looked irritated. "Some people are terribly selfish. Would they really give us a lower rating if we moved them? Even if you threw in a free dinner or something?"

"I could comp their stay," I said, knowing he'd hate that. The Royal Suite and Owner's Suite were our most expensive rooms. We did sometimes comp a night but not typically more than one.

Floyd shook his head. "I guess I'll settle for the Owner's Suite then."

I got him set up and then asked if he needed any assistance with his luggage. Unsurprisingly, he said yes. He'd booked for a week, which made my heart sink. A full week of Floyd. And without warning. I watched as he crooked a finger at one of the bellhops to bring his luggage over. Of course, he'd already found someone to help with his luggage.

As he headed towards the elevators, I took in a deep breath to calm my nerves, thinking about what a nightmare of a week this would be. At the same time, Olive walked out of my office. She is very considerate when she's in a public place by trying not to look as if she just popped in. Even so, the chill of having a ghost come up behind you is startling and did nothing for my nerves. I practically jumped.

Just then, the phone rang. Suzanne picked up.

"It's the woman in 785. The ghost appeared!" Olive practically clapped her hands.

I would have shared her joy if I hadn't just checked Floyd in. We'd been trying to figure out if there really was a ghost in the room or not. People had asked about it, but none of my workers nor Olive had ever seen the ghost.

But my lack of enthusiasm required that Olive ask why I wasn't more excited about the news, which meant I had to tell her.

"Floyd Bowman showed up unannounced."

"Oh dear," Olive said, her mouth turning down. She fingered the strand of faux pearls that was eternally around her neck over the peach twinset she always wore. Olive had worked with Floyd so she understood what I meant.

"That was poor timing, wasn't it?" she finally added.

I nodded as I heard the elevator door ding. I glanced over and Floyd was marching back to the desk looking thunderous.

Chapter Two

Despite the music playing in the background, I fancied I could hear the heels of Floyd's shoes clacking on the floor. No squeaks for him. The smell of pizza receded into the background and I was assailed with the sickly sweet stink of my own sweat while I tried to figure out what I might have done to get Floyd so up in arms. This was what my boss did to me.

"Stop being a ninny," Olive snipped next to me. "He's only one of your bosses. The worst of them, really."

"Should you be here?" I asked.

Floyd didn't believe in ghosts. Even if he thought the woman beside me resembled his deceased former manager, he'd think it was just a look-a-like and nothing was going to deter him from such a theory. Even if Olive popped out in front of him.

Olive, knowing Floyd as she did, chose to wander into my office before disappearing. I hoped that in his mood, Floyd hadn't noticed her. Him deciding to yell at me for having a stranger behind the desk was all that I needed. Oddly, while Olive wore the clothing she'd worn the day before she died, she did not have her hotel employee badge on. I wondered if that had any significance.

"Mr. Bowman, what's happened?" I asked cordially.

"Your bell-girl or bell-person or whatever she wants to be called dropped my luggage on the ground and did not apologize for it," he snapped. "I expect that you'll be training your employees to treat guests with better care."

"I believe they like to be called bellhops, it's more gender neutral," I explained. "And I'll be sure to let the door manager to know about the problem. Did you get a name?"

"Of course I didn't get a name! As if I, as a guest, have to go to the trouble to get names when you ought to know them all! You're the manager!" Floyd pointed at me, his finger getting closer and closer to my face all the time. I was thankful for the wide, chest high desk that stood between us. Fortunately, I hadn't chosen to move over to the lower area where we served those in wheelchairs.

"I should know, of course," I said. "Usually I do, but I was rather flustered by your appearance."

I hoped that the smile I gave him looked like a smile and not like a grimace.

"You're needed up in Suite 785," Suzanne broke in, putting down the phone.

"Probably another unhappy guest. If this is the way you run the hotel, I'll be looking for another manager!" Floyd snapped and turned on his heel.

"Sorry?" Suzanne said. "It just seemed that it was important you go now. The guest is scared because they saw the ghost."

"It's fine," I said. "I think Floyd tried to have Olive fired for most of her tenure here. I've only gotten him up in arms twice now. So long as the other siblings outlive him, I don't have anything to worry about. They don't want to have to hire a new hotel manager."

Suzanne still looked worried. Olive reappeared.

"I'll kill him off in my next book," she said.

"You aren't even finished with this one!" I exclaimed. In January we'd had a conference of cozy mystery writers at the hotel. Olive had decided she wanted to write a mystery. As a ghost she couldn't hold a pen or type on a computer, but we'd managed to work out a way that she could dictate her book and Suzanne would upload it into a program that would transcribe it. Then Suzanne would go through and correct any of the most major mistakes the transcription program made before consulting with Olive.

"Actually," Olive said, smiling. "I finished yesterday. Suzanne has already had the last part uploaded. Now we get to edit." She rubbed her hands together as if she were a villain about to foil a plot.

"Congratulations!" I said. While I'd had concerns about the whole project, mostly worried that Olive would drive Suzanne to distraction and she'd quit to avoid my erstwhile friend, it had worked out surprisingly well. Olive had been in a good mood, sharing long stories about her process with me in the evenings. It was a nice change from her listening to me and asking me all sorts of questions about what had happened in the hotel every day. As if she missed much. Usually, when something happened, she'd pop in to hear all about it.

Olive walked with me to the elevator and got inside still bubbling about her book being done. I would have thought she'd be more excited about the ghost, seeing she'd popped in to warn me about it. Chances were Floyd had her as up in arms as he had me.

"I can't wait to see how much Suzanne likes it. She's said very nice things about it, though she says that sometimes my language is rather dated." Olive sniffed as if such a thing weren't possible.

"I know there are terms my younger workers use that I don't," I said. "Language is always changing. So long as your sleuth is of an age to use that language, it shouldn't be a problem."

"I think I'd be nearly a hundred if I were still alive. I can't recall exactly..." Olive trailed off. I knew that she didn't always remember her life all that clearly but certain things stood out. I wondered if it bothered her to not know exactly how old she was.

"It's understandable that some of your phrases might be a bit old fashioned. Let Suzanne help you doctor those up," I said. "Easy enough." At least I hoped so. I mean, I didn't want to be getting Suzanne into more trouble.

The elevator let us off on the seventh floor. This floor had blue carpet with gray speckles. I'd not gone for anything red or burgundy on the floor as I worried it would look too much like blood. While I advertised this as a haunted hotel, I wanted people to feel as if those deaths had taken place long ago.

Many hotels had deaths in them, but I didn't want minds going to murder. Bad enough that we actually had one murder here in January. No one needed to be reminded of that with shades of red in the carpet like blood spatter. Of course, perhaps that was me. I did read a fair number of police procedurals and I loved crime drama shows.

Room 785 was a suite and was set a few doors down from the elevator. Convenient but quieter than if it were right across the way. When we'd updated the elevators last, I'd made sure they were as quiet as they could be. I didn't want guests complaining about their experiences.

I knocked on the door. Jean opened the door looking

paler than she had when she'd checked in. Her smartly trimmed gray hair was mussed as if she'd run her hands through it.

"I didn't believe it, really," she whispered. "I've had things happen but I've never seen a ghost!"

"Is it still around?" I asked.

"He disappeared for a bit and then oozed through the door about a minute ago. If it had been sooner, I couldn't have brought myself to answer your knock." She shivered.

Considering the chill in the doorway, I doubted it was a dramatic shiver. Cold spots were common around ghosts. I was used to feeling the chill from Olive. I doubted that Jean's ghost had made it as cold as it felt now. No doubt Olive's chill and the ghost's were feeding each other.

"May I come in?" I asked.

"Oh. Sorry." Jean stepped aside.

This particular suite was more of a mini-suite. The room was large with a sofa near the window and the bed up closest to the bathroom. Instead of the tub/shower combo most rooms had, this one had a walk-in shower and a separate soaking tub, though it wasn't a huge soaking tub. Those were reserved for the larger suites.

The view looked out over the back of the hotel and the trees that clustered around the landscape. Up close, I knew you could look down and see one of the hiking trails that went behind the hotel and around to the pool. In summer, sometimes I walked that trail to be sure I got some sunlight. I tended to spend so much time running around inside that I'd forget to get out.

The ghost stood near that window looking out. Like many ghosts, he appeared as if he were an ordinary human being. I noted he wore jeans and a polo shirt in faded yellow. I didn't know if he just didn't appear as solid as most ghosts or if his shirt had been that faded when he wore it.

I'd learned that all ghosts had different abilities. Olive, for instance, could wander around the hotel as much as she wanted but other ghosts were isolated to a single place. ABC Smithers, as I called the ghost in the restaurant, only ever appeared there. Sometimes he stayed in the attic and sometimes down in the restaurant proper. Clara was a maid in the hotel and she ran down the hallway in the basement on a fairly regular basis.

Another ghost, Angus, only ever showed up in a storm peering in the windows from outside. Rumor had it, he'd frozen to death in a snowstorm just outside the hotel.

Smithers periodically spoke but didn't talk the way Olive did. Olive, so far as I knew had the most ability to talk and to wander around. She claimed she couldn't leave the hotel but sometimes I wondered if she just didn't want to. The world around here had changed since she died.

"Hello?" I said, approaching the ghost. I noticed that Jean stayed well back, still shivering. Olive, however, followed me, looking interested.

"Hello," he said, turning.

He didn't look particularly old. The planes of his face were harsh and unforgiving. His eyes appeared even more so. The tone of the hello was more one of annoyance than pleasure at talking with someone.

"Who are you?" I asked.

He sniffed. It sounded like something Floyd would do upon being asked who he was.

"You'd think the hotel would have that sort of information on guests," he said. He didn't appear to notice Jean, or if he did, he wasn't willing to admit it.

"I just got up here," I said.

The ghost looked at Olive. "You checked me in!"

While that wasn't super helpful, it at least gave us a timeline.

"I tend to forget things like that," Olive said. "Being dead and all."

The ghost frowned.

"I didn't like you then, either. You were a haughty one. Did you kill me?"

"Me?" Olive appeared taken aback.

"You certainly threatened to," the ghost said.

"Who are you?" I demanded. I didn't like how he was treating Olive. I couldn't imagine her threatening a guest. I'd worked with her for a couple of years before becoming manager. Olive could be very particular, but she wasn't mean.

"Corbin Moore." He held out a hand and then looked at it, frowning, pulling it back as if he realized that as a ghost he probably couldn't touch me. "And you?"

"I'm Maggie Davenport, the hotel manager," I said.

"Hope you're nicer than that one," he pointed at Olive.

Olive, for her part humphed and played with her pearls. She was surprisingly quiet around Corbin.

"I need to go," he said suddenly and drifted past us. When he got to the door, he just disappeared.

"Is he gone?" Jean asked. "For real?"

She had apparently missed the part about Olive admitting to being dead as she looked from one of us to the other.

"For now," I said. "We've spent a great deal of time trying to find out about him. I don't think he shows up much. Perhaps it's the day?"

Jean started nodding. She went to her luggage and picked up a few notes. "Yes. Some ghosts only appear on the day they died. No one explained why but it's just how they are."

"I didn't know that," I said.

"Really?" Jean looked at me in surprise. As if just because I ran a haunted hotel, I knew all about ghosts. In reality, while I had picked up a few things, I was not that knowledgeable about them. Olive was my main source for trustworthy information. Everything else I thought I knew was just guesswork, though Olive admitted she was often guessing as well, but based on her own experience.

"Really."

After that, I said my goodbyes, with Olive trailing along, looking thoughtful. Out in the hallway, Jean's door safely closed I paused and looked at her.

"You were quiet in there."

"I don't remember him," Olive said.

"You've said you've forgotten a lot. Maybe he's one of those things." I didn't understand why she was bothered by this.

"He thinks I threatened him. Like maybe I murdered him! You'd think that would be something I'd remember," she said.

"To be honest, threatening a guest is not something I'd expect from you. I did work with you for a few years." And getting used to having my old boss popping in around the place had taken quite a bit of getting used to. People tell me I should get out more and make more friends, but this was the kind of thing that happened to me when I knew people.

"But that was later," Olive said.

"Dish." I stopped near the elevator and crossed my arms. I did not push the down button, so we were going to stand in front of the three silver doors until she spoke. I hoped she wouldn't get angry and just pop out.

Olive sighed and shook her head.

"I had a drinking problem right after my divorce. It's

not something I like to talk about but it's true. A few times I was less than professional with some of the more difficult guests. Fortunately, Ari Bowman stepped in and got me into treatment. She was always the kindest of the Bowman family. Floyd wanted to fire me. I think he still would if he knew I hung around as a ghost."

"And yet you're right there in front of him and he doesn't notice."

"Floyd only notices what he wants to. If he knew and believed I was still here as a ghost, he'd probably hire an exorcist," Olive said. "Once he takes against you, he won't ever back down."

"I've just always ignored his outbursts. The others have to agree to fire me," I said.

"That was always my take. Ari liked me. I think she felt a kinship of sorts," Olive said. "But if Corbin was a guest during that time, then I could easily have gone off on him. He seems like the pompous type doesn't he? My ex-husband was that way."

"I never knew you were married." Olive hadn't ever talked about it.

"I was. For about ten years. I didn't always live in the apartment. In fact, Ari designed it when I was in treatment. She felt that if I were on site, I would be less likely to start overindulging again because there would always be something to distract me. Before, I lived in town. Up in Singing Vale Heights."

I gave Olive a side-eye look. Singing Vale Heights was the nicest part of town. If I were British, I'd say posh. It deserved such a word. The houses were older, mostly sixties and seventies style homes and they were large by those standards, but not necessarily today's. Maybe two thousand square feet on one or two floors. But each had a large property of several acres mostly tucked in around forests.

The community was gated, though trying to fence the space that the Heights covered was impossible, so it was more symbolic. Much less symbolic were the guard houses that sat at the entrance and towards the center of the area and the guards that drove around in large black SUVs decorated with Singing Vale Heights Security on the doors and dark tint on the windows.

"I could have had the house. It was different back then," Olive said. "But who would want to live in such a monstrosity all alone. He left with a younger woman and moved down to Florida. I heard he died about a decade before I did. I treated myself to cake and ice cream that night and thanked my stars that he left me. I had had no idea how unhappy I'd become."

I nodded. That was about as personal as I'd ever heard Olive talk.

"I can't believe I might have murdered someone and no one ever knew," Olive whispered. "I feel terrible, sort of. But also rather proud that I was such a bad ass."

I turned to press the black button with the down arrow so that Olive wouldn't see me trying not to laugh at her description of herself. Olive was bossy and sure of herself, but I had a hard time seeing her as a bad ass. And no matter what she said, I suspect that even drunk she was more likely to throw a glass at someone, stamp her feet, and perhaps verbally assault them than actually murder them.

Chapter Three

The lobby area was busy when I returned. Mark, my daytime front desk supervisor, and Suzanne my main desk worker, were both busily helping people. Two part-timers were also working with guests to check them in. The smell of pizza was nearly drowned out by the human smells of floral perfumes, spicy after-shaves, both covering lightly sweating bodies. It wasn't quite a gym, but nearly there.

Our air-fresheners were no doubt working over-time.

The fireplace had no fire nor had it for the last week. We'd had sunny and unseasonably warm weather which meant that no one was really in the mood to cuddle by the flames. I liked the ambiance of the lobby better when it was lit. Without it, the large windows and the shiny white flooring made the place feel cold, even when it was hot outside. The orangish flames flickering against the black interior surrounded by the stone outer portion made the whole place feel warmer and cozier, more like the mountain lodge décor I preferred.

Floyd would have done away with the stone fireplace and put in a central round fireplace in silver metal. The very idea made my stomach turn. Fortunately, not all of the Bowmans had such bad taste and he was easily outvoted on that one.

The music from the bar was louder now, too. Of course, so were the people talking and laughing. The people who had checked in on prior days or even earlier this afternoon were chatting with friends, old and new. Looking over at the bar, I recognized a few people from town.

Olive had disappeared before the elevator doors opened so I walked towards the desk alone.

There wasn't another terminal free. I checked with each person to be sure they didn't need me to do anything before I slipped into my office. There was only one person waiting for assistance and I hoped that he wouldn't be too offended that I didn't immediately begin helping him. I needed a terminal to do so and there wasn't one.

While I felt a little guilty about not helping out at the front desk. I did appreciate the time to be able to do a bit of searching on Corbin Moore. Unfortunately, he'd died long enough ago that there wasn't a whole lot to find online, though I kept at it until the conversation outside died down and Mark peeked his head in to say good-night.

My stomach growled and I knew it was time to go down and have a bite to eat and talk with my cats. I have two lovely Siamese cats who live with me. They were no doubt wondering where their dinner was. Normally, I went down earlier and got them settled.

I went down the stairs to the basement rather than taking an elevator. I didn't want to wait nor did I want our guests to have to wait any longer than necessary for an elevator to take them up to their rooms. Besides, it was good exercise.

While I might be heading down to a basement, the

stairwell was light and airy. The designers had made it that way to keep people from feeling as if they were heading partially below ground. Add to that, with the large windows in the conference room across the way, when the doors were open, it was nearly as bright an airy as the lobby upstairs.

I turned to my right to walk down the hallway. I heard Floyd's grating voice talking more loudly than normal. I paused to draw in a breath and calm myself.

"That's not something I'll do." That voice belonged to my security guard, Jake. "You're nuts. And that's a hill I'm willing to die on."

Jake's voice was raised slightly with fury behind his words. I had no idea what Floyd had just asked of him but at that moment I was willing to stand behind my head of security.

"And you just might," Floyd snarled.

"Is that a threat?" Jake growled. The anger in it made me take a small step back, my heart thudding.

"A promise," Floyd snapped.

"I think you'll find that I'm not one who takes threats well," Jake replied, his voice slightly more even but the low tones made the comment sound more threatening than it should have. "There's a reason I'm in security."

I heard footsteps going down the stairs to the subbasement. Soon enough my ears picked up the whoosh of the employee elevator doors. Someone got inside.

Even then, I paused a bit longer. I really did not want to run into Floyd after he'd just had a run in with someone. I liked Jake. He was solid, or so I thought. I knew there was something about anger management issues in his background but he'd never had a problem before. Of course, talking to Floyd, I'd sound like I had anger issues.

My stomach growled again and I headed down the

hallway to my apartment, pointedly not looking towards the employee elevator as I passed. I did not want to see either of the men still there. I never wanted to see Floyd, certainly not after he had had words with someone. And, although Jake and I got along, I had a feeling that he needed time to cool down.

I unlocked my door. Once inside I leaned back against it feeling the solidity of it. This was my sanctuary. While the living area wasn't large, it was comfortable, particularly when I had the gas fireplace on. I enjoyed evenings with my cats, curled on my sofa watching my television.

Chai and Latte were both standing on the sofa, Chai still stretching from his long afternoon nap. Latte gave me a loud meow letting me know that they were overdue to be fed. The two Siamese leaped down in sync and then began to twine around my legs, Chai from right to left and Latte from left to right. They made it almost impossible for me to move.

I bent down and rubbed their backs which settled them a little. To be honest it settled me even more.

Having gotten them their food, I made myself some dinner. I had never been much of a cook and I wasn't about to start that night. Grilled cheese and a small salad would do. I had some cut-up fruit for dessert. When I'd finished my meal and the apartment smelled nicely of bread being toasted in a fry pan, I settled in to do some more sleuthing on Corbin Moore.

I tried obituaries but found nothing. The local paper was online and they'd employed someone to put the back issues online as well. Those were images rather than typed in, so probably not searchable. I went to their site and began to paw through the information.

Olive hadn't told me when she'd gotten divorced. I had to guess at the year. It would have been well before I started, but after she'd been at the hotel long enough for Ari to take a liking to her. And, Olive and her husband had been in town long enough to purchase a house in a nice area. Surely, they would have rented at first, or purchased a starter home.

I made some guesses and started around 1973. I learned more about lost pets and ancient local politics than I cared to know. It was interesting that our local grocer had expanded and built the building that I thought was old in 1974. Not that that helped me with my sleuthing, but learning about the town's background was the sort of thing that kept me going.

The father of one my security guards won an award at the science fair which made me smile sadly. Brandon, my security guard, had to watch his father regularly because he was in the early stages of dementia. The man was younger than I was based on the dates. And here he'd been so good at science.

I pushed my maudlin mulling away and kept on skimming through the papers.

Chai came up and settled next to me once he realized that the laptop wasn't going anywhere. Latte came up and settled next to his brother. He placed a paw on my hip as if pushing me away but I knew it was so he, too, could be close to me. The two cats were good at that.

They started grooming and then some mutual grooming went on before they completely settled in. I still had not come upon anything about Corbin Moore. I would have thought that if he had died, the newspaper would have reported it. Of course, perhaps Olive had worked there longer than I thought. I still had almost twenty years to go before I began my work at the Neary-Ten.

I continued on through. I learned that Suzanne's

family had made a huge donation to the local high school back then. I wondered if she knew and if that was something she was proud of. I also wondered if she ever intended to leave the area.

Mark's family was also local, though their appearances in the paper tended to be in the crime log. Fortunately, Mark had been a manager for a very long time and I knew I could trust him no matter his family's background.

Finally, I found a small blurb about a man dying in a car accident. The police weren't certain of what caused it and they were investigating. The man's name was Corbin Moore. I noted the date of the issue. Today was the anniversary of his death. Apparently, Jean was onto something.

He'd died in the morning. I kept reading. They were considering suicide as there appeared to be no other reason for his car to go off the road as it did. No mention was made if he'd been drinking. Perhaps because it was early morning, they'd decided against getting a tox screen. Of course, that was long ago. Those might not have been so as often.

A police officer, no doubt long retired, was quoted as saying, "There are some inconsistencies in the crash that suggest this was not just a single car accident. However, without witnesses or other evidence, we have no way to know exactly what happened. It's likely that if there was another car, it has long since left the area."

I closed the laptop and pulled at my lip. Interesting. If Olive did do it, she could have been driving under the influence. Perhaps that was what made her accept Ari's suggestion that she go into treatment. Maybe the guilt over what she had done was the reason she haunted the hotel.

Olive was my best friend there. For a long time, I would have said she was my only real friend. However, after the murder this winter, I'd been working on coming out of my shell and slowing decreasing the distance I'd kept between myself as the boss and my employees. I had realized I needed living friends. No matter how many living friends I found, however, I didn't want to lose my best friend.

Chapter Four

I didn't see Olive at all the next morning. She often showed up as I got my day started. We'd also normally talk while I ate dinner. Now she was busy editing her book with Suzanne. There were times when I felt a bit jealous of the time Suzanne spent with her, but mostly I made sure that I appreciated the private time.

Suzanne and I went to lunch regularly now. I also spent time training at the martial arts center, or dojo as the regulars called it, on Mondays. Dori, one of my restaurant workers, had gotten me involved in the self-defense courses and then jiu jitsu. After my experience with a killer last winter, I wanted to be able to protect myself. I wasn't at all confident that the classes had helped, but I'd met a few people there. Some, like Alyssa at the front desk, and Dori my employee, I quite liked. Others, like a woman named Teena, who was only a decade or so younger but acted like a twenty year old, flirting with any man who came in, were less agreeable.

Not that I was worried about not having many friends. I liked the quiet life. In fact, I had to push myself to leave on Mondays for martial arts. I liked my apartment and my own company far too much.

Work was a different story. It was part of my routine. I took my coffee with me and headed upstairs to get back to work. Addy would be trading off shifts with Suzanne who would cover for a few hours until Mark arrived. He usually stayed late so there was a manager there at all times, except for the short period when I was on call but not at the front desk. Actually, I was always on call, but I had good staff who kept the place running for me when I wasn't actually on shift.

The bar wasn't open so the lobby played soft instrumental versions of 80s pop music. When I was young, we used to call the instrumental version of the music of the 50s elevator music. Now it was my music that played in elevators. I sighed. Just another sign of getting old.

I waved at Suzanne and went into my office to set my coffee down. I took another sip, savoring the bitter flavor and then headed out to the desk to see what was going on. The desk was large and had four stations for checking people in and out. Normally that was more than enough but sometimes, such as when there was a conference of some sort, we could get a line. A number of years ago, we'd begun having automatic checkout for people and that had made mornings much quieter. It was why the early morning shift was the one without a manager on duty.

"Anything?" I asked Suzanne.

She shook her head.

"Good. Floyd hasn't found something wrong, then," I said.

Suzanne gave me a tight smile.

"What is it?" I asked.

"I heard him last night when I was down in the small conference room Olive and I use for editing. We were talking about something and Floyd was down there yelling at someone. I didn't hear another voice, so he must have been on his phone."

"When was that? I know he had words with Jake about the time I went down for dinner, around six-thirty."

"It was after that. Olive and I worked until about eight and this was just before we decided to pack up. Olive said his blathering kept her from thinking straight. She didn't care about her killer and victim, she just wanted to take Floyd out." Suzanne sort of giggled.

"I haven't seen her this morning," I said.

"Neither have I," Suzanne said. "But she'll pop in when she wants to."

I nodded, wondering if I should share with her what I learned about Olive and the car accident. Of course, Olive was private. If she wanted Suzanne to know about her history, she'd tell her. I needed to wait until she showed up. Perhaps if I let her know how Corbin had died, she'd remember something, like perhaps hitting another car after she'd been drinking. Of course, that didn't seem like the kind of thing you'd forget, but who knew with ghosts?

Instead, I changed the subject and asked Suzanne how the book was going.

"Olive is taking the changes I've suggested better than I expected," Suzanne said. "I told her I read a lot in the genre so she's happy to listen. I've always thought of her as…"

Trailing off Suzanne glanced around.

"She tells me she can't hear unless she's visible," I said, reading her reaction.

"Kind of bossy." Suzanne still kept her voice low, leaning towards me as we stood near the desk.

Out of the corner of my eye I noticed a guest coming out of the elevator. She headed towards us at the desk. I backed up so that Suzanne could take care of her. Sometimes someone wanted a printed receipt to make sure they were checked out.

It was time to stop gossiping and worrying about Olive and get to work.

"There is a stink in my room," a tall, dark-haired woman said. She was dressed in designer label clothing, though it was casual enough for a hike through our woods. Her dark hair was styled perfectly, though unfortunately it was too early for her to have gone to our spa to have it done. She'd have created the look herself. I wondered how long it took. The intricate curls that hung down from an updo appeared to be quite a lot of work. Of course, if she were lucky, perhaps she just pulled her hair up and it did that naturally.

My hair would just frizz and half fall out of any bun I attempted, leaving me looking as if I'd just wrestled a bear and barely walked out with my life.

"I'll have someone go up and check it out," Suzanne said. She typed something into the computer. My maintenance crew could fix most anything and if they couldn't, I did have a couple of rooms available to move someone to, depending upon the level of her choice.

"Your name and room number?" Suzanne asked.

I listened. Her name was Catalina Thomas and she was staying in one of our regular rooms that were interspersed between the large suites on the top floor. In fact, she was next to Floyd. If there was a smell up there, I was surprised that he hadn't come down and complained about it.

Of course, I'd long suspected that Floyd had a drug habit. He could easily be up there sleeping and hadn't yet noticed it. Hopefully, Catalina's complaint would allow us to find the source and get it taken care of before he woke up. Even if he still noticed it, we could say that we'd taken care of the problem already.

Floyd might not appreciate that it happened at all, but at least he couldn't say I didn't take care of things once I'd been informed. I'd make a note in my managerial report about the complaint and note that someone was going up immediately.

"Will you be going out for a bit? And is it okay for us to enter?" Suzanne asked out front.

"I will go to breakfast, I suppose. You have the café?" Catalina pointed down the hall towards where we had a nice little café that served breakfast, lunch, and light dinner items. They served burgers, sandwiches and soups. For breakfast, we went all out with a variety of breakfast items. Later in the day, guests had the choice of the café, the bars, and the fancier dinner restaurants which was why the later menu was so limited.

"We do," Suzanne smiled.

"Afterwards, I was wondering about the sights in town," Catalina said.

In my office, I double checked that maintenance had gotten Suzanne's request for someone to check out Catalina's room.

I listened as Suzanne told her about the highlights of our little town. It wasn't much. I mean we had one main street. We had an old cemetery that many people like to look around and the downtown was listed as an historic district. We had a museum that could fit inside one of the bars in the hotel but apparently it was rather unique and people enjoyed walking through it.

On the weekends, two elderly women opened up a small store front museum which specialized in hauntings. They'd started it once I began to market the hotel as haunted. I guess they were local ghost hunters and loved all things paranormal. The little museum and associated books and items made them a tidy little sum and kept them busy.

Ghost hunters, of course, often visited the Cornered Reader to see if that local ghost was around, but not everyone noticed him. Ghosts tend to look like ordinary people but for a bit of a chill and perhaps doing something odd. The ghost there just sat in one of the chairs and watched the world go by, or engaged in a bit of a chat with anyone who sat with him. Most people thought he was an old guy hanging out, which I suppose wasn't wrong. They just didn't understand he was dead.

It was no wonder the ghost hunters loved having conferences here. Between the cemetery, the museum, the bookstore, and our hotel, we had a plethora of hauntings. And it was far quieter than Savannah, which I'd heard could get very crowded in the summer, not to mention quite hot.

My desk phone rang, my direct line. I picked it up.

"This is Maggie," I said.

"Not finding anything wrong in the room," a male voice said.

I asked a few questions ascertaining that I was talking to my maintenance person and that they were in Catalina's room.

"I think the smell is coming from the Owner's Suite."

My stomach sank to my knees. I did not want to have to disturb Floyd. But perhaps he'd appreciate that someone smelled something in the hallway and I was being proactive.

"Is there a sign on the door of the Owner's Suite?" I asked.

"Nope," Maintenance said.

"Knock and see if anyone answers. Maybe he went down for an early breakfast."

Floyd hadn't come down to complain so I'd be surprised if he had. He tried to never miss an opportunity to show his superior powers of observation and potentially business acumen. The only reason he got away with things like that was because neither Olive nor I was particularly competitive about our jobs. We did them well and knew it. But we weren't seeking to become the manager of a different hotel. The Neary-Ten and all its quirks suited us.

More importantly, we only had to put up with him once or twice a year and usually we had plenty of warning. Floyd, or any of the Bowmans, just dropping in like this was nearly unheard of. I'd have to ask Olive if he'd ever just dropped in when she was in charge.

Speaking of, I drummed my fingers on my desk wondering where she'd gotten off to. It was unlike her to remain out of sight for so long, particularly when there were questions to be asked. Of course, she might be wherever ghosts went racking her brain trying to remember if she'd really murdered Corbin Moore.

I found a sharpie and wrote on a large piece of paper which I left on the top of my desk.

"Olive, when you see this, find me. Important."

While she couldn't hear anyone when she was invisible, I knew she could see things. It was a discussion we'd had before. Fortunately, I suspected Olive was kind enough not to be secretly watching me while I was indisposed in the bathroom. Otherwise, I'd have had to move out.

She'd once told me that she'd been looking for me and had found the cats using the litter box which she'd been terribly embarrassed by, so I was fairly certain that she'd have avoided me until the end of my days if she'd ever accidentally found me bathing or something.

The phone on my desk rang again. I almost never got calls on it, so I was surprised. The maintenance person must either be in trouble with Floyd or he'd found the source of the stink.

"This is Maggie."

"You need to get up to the Owner's Suite." The man's voice shook and he sounded near tears. This did not bode well.

Chapter Five

The upper floor was quiet. Because our best suites were on that floor, the carpet was a brighter blue and had small green and cream splotches on it. At one time it had felt more festive and higher end. Now it looked cheap to me, but perhaps I was seeing it through Floyd's eyes. Of course, unless it had been made of solid gold, he'd have claimed it look cheap.

The walls were cream with white wainscoting which remained in excellent condition. The paintings along the walls were all images from around the Appalachians, and because the images were all tree heavy, they picked up the green flecks in the carpet nicely.

The HVAC came on startling me. The floor was far too quiet, but the air had been getting rather stuffy. The newlyweds were in the Royal Suite towards the opposite end of the hallway. The Owner's Suite was on the end closer to the elevators.

The owners talked about re-designing the place and moving the elevators to the other side of the lobby so they were more central. However, when they'd overbuilt the old building, they'd stayed with the elevators in the place where they were, which was not very central. Some day I'd love to have another bank, perhaps on the other side of the lobby but that wouldn't be happening any time soon. We might be in the black, but we weren't making money hand over fist.

I had to admit people seemed happy enough to put up with our limitations and seemed content with their lodgings. Now and then I'd find a complaint about long waits for the elevators, but overall, our guests seemed to absorb the limitations with good grace and said very little.

Floyd, however, made it sound like he had always been for moving the elevators, though I knew from Olive that she'd been the only voice of reason, suggesting they didn't want to add five floors and if they did, they needed to add more elevator banks.

I sighed, wishing Olive would show up. I was beginning to grow a bit worried. What if she had killed Corbin Moore, either accidentally or on purpose, and now, having realized that, and met him again, she'd moved on. Olive had admitted she didn't know why some people stayed around as spirits and others didn't. What if having worked out some grave sin, Olive no longer needed to stay? I'd be lost without her friendship.

Building new friends took time. Now that I thought about it, Olive had been around to work with Suzanne after she met the spirit Corbin Moore, so unless she'd had a major aha moment, she was probably just off wherever ghosts went to and hadn't popped back in.

I reached the Owner's Suite. A man in dark blue overalls, the usual uniform of our maintenance personnel, stood by the door, dancing from foot to foot. His red hair was cropped short and the freckles on his face stood out in stark relief to the paleness of his skin. I couldn't remember his name, but fortunately he had his name tag on which said his name was Paul.

"What do I need to see?" I asked.

The door was open. I noticed a light on in the room and the curtains still closed. The maids hadn't been up there yet, but it was still early. Mark had just been arriving when I'd gone upstairs. I smelled something pungent, as if the toilet had backed up and spilled solid contents all over the floor. Underlying it was something vaguely metallic and almost rotten. It was more than a little unpleasant. I had to admire Catalina's fortitude in calmly reporting the problem if it was anywhere near as bad in her room.

Paul just pointed, not going in with me.

I wondered what Floyd could have done.

To my right as I entered was a large walk-through closet that ended at the large bathroom. Floyd had brought only a single carry-on suitcase and that was on the bench in the walk-through, open. He'd hung up a single shirt and a pair of nice trousers.

Lights were on in the bathroom, the white tile reflecting off of them. Nothing appeared out of place. The smell was stronger when I entered the big sitting area.

The suite was silent, the HVAC not having come on in there. It felt stuffy, though. On the left wall were the controls and I noted that the air had been turned completely off and the heat turned on, but without the fan. That was strange. I couldn't image that Floyd wouldn't have wanted to stay comfortable. I hoped he hadn't gotten sick, although that would explain the smell.

The main part of the room was large, with a sofa and a television in the sitting area. The television was against the far wall, which had two large openings into an alcove that held the bed and dressers. A bottle of wine and two glasses sat on the coffee table, one glass on its side, though it hadn't broken.

I frowned, wondering what had happened. I stepped further in, and peered first into the bathroom from that end, but everything appeared to be in place. No sludge oozed from the toilet. In fact, other than a toiletry case, nothing appeared to even have been touched.

Stepping back out, I looked into the bed alcove. There was the source of the smell. Floyd lay on his side, naked. Something reddish brown soiled the sheets and had dripped onto the carpet making the blood spatter pattern that I'd so carefully avoided on the carpets.

I gasped, my heart thudding.

To add insult to injury, Olive chose that moment to pop in. I jumped, gasping slightly. Up to that moment I'd been reasonably calm at having found my most hated employer dead in my hotel. Perhaps I'd been in shock and Olive appearing had brought me out of it. She certainly made me shiver with her chill.

"I noticed this shortly before your maintenance person came in. I was about to go down and tell you, but Mr. Maintenance pulled out his cell phone and called."

"Did he call the police as well?" I whispered.

"I don't believe so," Olive said. "I didn't see him make more than one call. I didn't hear him call you, but about the time I got to your office you had left so I figured you were coming here."

"I've been worried about you," I said.

"As if I'd do this?" Olive asked. "I mean, now that I'm dead, if I could have, I might have."

The look I gave her must have been surprised or perhaps judgmental.

She rolled her eyes at me. "Just Floyd. He's always been so annoying."

I nodded, backing out of the room, remembering all the lessons from hundreds of crime show episodes and murder mystery novels. I shouldn't touch anything and I shouldn't move anything. You never knew what could be a clue.

Chapter Six

The police took very little time to arrive. It worried me that they were so prompt. The first on the scene was a tall, stocky older man in uniform. He arrived within five minutes of my call. When you consider that we're down the highway from town and along a long road that pretty much goes nowhere but the hotel, his arrival was faster than I expected. Of course, perhaps he'd been sitting along the highway looking for speeders and this call sounded far more interesting.

He stepped inside and took a look at Floyd, making sure he was dead. As if I could have missed that. While I admit that I am not doctor, Floyd's body was messed up enough that even the most cursory glance should have told him the condition. The patrolman got on his radio and repeated my call.

The patrolman asked Paul and I to wait. Olive had pointedly disappeared before he arrived, startling Paul. Apparently, he was new or he'd managed to not encounter any of our ghosts before. The patrolman kept staring at us as if we were suspects, so I didn't feel comfortable making polite talk with the young maintenance worker.

"Can we go sit in the chairs out by the elevator?" I asked nicely.

"Best if you stay here, ma'am, in case the detectives have any questions."

I sighed. The stink from Floyd's room was getting to me. It seemed awfully strong if he'd been killed within the day. And he'd been downstairs yesterday afternoon so it would have been just a few hours ago. Suzanne had mentioned hearing him talking on the phone or at the very least having a one-sided conversation around 8 PM last night. She hadn't seen him, so she couldn't be absolutely certain.

Jake would be able to place Floyd near the employee elevator a bit earlier, though. Perhaps they'd talked about what Floyd wanted to do. To annoy Jake, it had to have something to do with security. Something that Jake didn't think could or should be done. I'd have to talk to him.

Paul hummed softly under his breath. Either he was a poor hummer or it was a strange tune that I'd never heard. Given how out of touch I sometimes felt, it could have been either. The patrolman listened to his radio. He nodded a few times but said nothing.

Someone moved around in one of the rooms nearby. I hoped they wouldn't come out and find us all standing there. Of course, in a short time, I had a feeling this entire half of the floor was going to be filled with police. That was going to be a huge problem.

I texted Mark what was going on and to see if there would be a way to juggle rooms for anyone on this end of the hotel on the top floor. The floors below might be annoyed by sounds, but I'd wait until they complained. I had a feeling the police would prefer not to have to deal with guests coming in and out on this floor, though. I wanted to get a head start on figuring out how we could compensate people for having to move them.

Finally, the elevator doors opened and I heard unfamiliar voices murmuring. A short, thin woman who looked more suited to playing Tinkerbell in the movies than being a police detective showed up. Her blonde hair was cut short and the large eyes in her rather pert face took in everything in a single glance.

She wore black jeans and blue blouse that I guessed was short sleeved. A black blazer covered it so I couldn't see. She didn't look quite right in the outfit. I kept picturing her in a flowing skirt and boho top.

The man with her was taller, but that wasn't saying much. Average height and build, his brown hair made him extraordinarily nondescript. He looked me up and down and then Paul.

"What's up?" he asked the uniformed officer.

The woman snapped on gloves, more loudly but with a bit less finesse than the actors on television. If Olive were around, she'd say she was disappointed in her. Truth be told, so was I.

The detective did, however, pull out shoe coverings as well, before walking into the room. She stayed for some time while the other detective talked to the uniformed officer and took notes about the call, what he saw, where he'd been and who else had gone in the room.

The two of them turned to me and Paul.

I explained about the complaint we'd had about the smell from the room next door. I said I'd told Paul to check this room. I knew we had a guest, actually one of the owners, staying there, but had hoped that he wouldn't be too bothered. I nodded to Paul to take over the narrative.

It took him plenty of stops and starts to get to the point

where he'd seen Floyd. Paul had gone though the bath-room, expecting an over-flowing toilet in there. He went into far more detail than either I or the police needed about the problems involved in that. The detective's eyes glazed over. I thought the patrol officer was about to laugh before Paul figured that he should stick to what had actually happened and not the possible plumbing issues he'd been thinking about.

When Paul finally noticed the body on the bed, he'd stood shocked and left the room, calling me almost immediately.

I took up the narrative again, saying Paul had just told me to come up and I'd gone in and seen Floyd. It appeared he was dead so I'd left the room and called 911.

"What did you touch?" the detective asked.

"I might have touched the wall when I looked into the sleeping alcove," I said. "Probably the door and possibly the wall along entry hall."

He made notes. "We'll need both your prints to rule them out. Probably won't help. This is a hotel and it's either been cleaned or there will be tons of prints."

"There were two wine glasses on the coffee table. Floyd checked in alone. I don't know that he was meeting anyone here," I said.

"Floyd? You're on a first name basis with your guest?" the detective asked.

"He's one of the owners. Floyd Bowman."

The detective raised any eyebrow. It was finally getting through that Floyd wasn't an ordinary guest. An owner suggested someone with money or someone that the staff, perhaps didn't like.

"Was he planning to sell the place or something?"

"I have no idea," I said. The thought hadn't crossed my mind. It was doubtful. The Bowmans had a large portfolio with a variety of holdings. We were their only hotel, though, and from what I'd heard through the grapevine, several of them rather liked having one even if it wasn't their most profitable property. That might not have been true of Floyd, though.

"Normally, if something is going to change, we have a meeting with all the Bowmans," I said. "There are five children and each has an equal interest in the company. They all have to be in agreement to make changes to the holdings they have, which can take some time. I wouldn't expect that Floyd would come here unannounced with news like that."

The detective made note of that. "Do you know which of them I'd contact?"

"I'm not sure who," I said. "I do have contact information for each of them in my office downstairs."

He nodded. "I'll need that."

"Do you want me to forward it in an email or text it to you? Or do you prefer a printout?"

"Whichever," he said.

"When you saw him, were you sure it was Mr. Bowman and not someone visiting him?" the detective asked.

"It's Floyd. Unless it's someone who looks very much like him and is wearing the same suit that Floyd wore when he arrived." While I wasn't going to swear that the face under the blood was Floyd, it was definitely his suit. Besides, while Floyd was a jerk, it was difficult to see him murdering someone with a knife. He preferred to do his cutting with words.

"Is there anyone you know of who would want to harm Mr. Bowman?"

I sighed. The list was long.

"Floyd was rather difficult. To be honest, he was my least favorite of the Bowmans. He could find fault in anything which always put everyone on edge," I said. "He didn't come here often, but when he did, it helped to remember that he spoke quite critically to everyone."

The detective asked a few other questions which I answered as well as I could and handed me his card. Edward Penn. He didn't look like an Ed or an Eddie, but who knew?

"If we have more questions, we'll contact you," he said before turning to Paul.

I hesitated, wondering if I should stay with my employee while he was being questioned, but Detective Penn gave me a long look and waited until I got the hint to leave. As I walked off, I glanced back in time to see Detective Tinkerbell finally leaving the room. I so wanted to slip into one of the guest rooms and listen in but, unfortunately, the best ones were occupied, not to mention how it would have looked to the police.

With no other choice, I headed back down to my office to look up contact information for the other Bowman's.

Chapter Seven

Lunch time had arrived and the lobby area was a bit busier when I got back downstairs, still shaken by what I had seen. Music played from the lobby bar, an upbeat tune that felt out of place considering what had happened on the top floor. I hoped the police didn't find the music too distasteful. While the tune bothered me as I looked up the information on the Bowmans, I didn't call over to the bar to ask them to change it.

With any luck, most guests would miss the police who had come in, although looking out through our glass entry, I did see the large van that had pulled in which had "Crime Lab" written on the side in large letters. Not exactly what I wanted to see in our parking lot, but perhaps people would think they were visiting for lunch or something. Even as I had that thought, I laughed at myself. I was surprised more people weren't at the desk asking what was happening.

"What's going on?" Mark asked. Suzanne looked over from where she was talking to someone, clearly hoping to overhear.

I held up a finger for Mark so he knew I'd heard him and to wait.

Once the guest had finished their business and left the area by the desk, I told both Mark and Suzanne what had happened.

"The smell the woman reported earlier was from Floyd's room," I hissed, hoping that none of the guests who might be dining in the lobby bar had superhero hearing. "Maintenance found him dead."

"What?" Mark drew back, eyes wide.

Suzanne just stared with her jaw open.

"I had to come up with contact information for the rest of the family. Detective…" I pulled out his card to find his name. "Edward Penn wanted me to send him that information."

He hadn't said when, so I wasn't in a hurry. I mean, it was probably important but I doubted he'd be up there calling the family just like that. They'd send someone, of course, to the family home somewhere in New York, although I thought that Floyd had moved to California. Perhaps he had a wife and family, although if he did, I felt sorry for them. He was not someone I'd want to be married to.

"That's horrible," Suzanne finally said. "Who could have done such a thing?"

Olive wandered out from my office.

"I think the better question is who wouldn't have done such a thing," Olive said.

Mark started a bit. I noticed that since working with her, Olive no longer startled Suzanne.

"I mean he wasn't the easiest person to get along with, but I'm not sure many of us would have stooped to murder." I bit my lip, hoping what I said was true. I knew I hadn't. Mark had left that night, so he should be in the clear. I couldn't be certain about anyone else, though Olive and Suzanne alibied each other. And, as Olive said, she couldn't have because she couldn't handle physical objects.

"I might have," Olive said. "And I didn't like the way that detective was eyeing you. I mean, Floyd did give you a difficult time, practically threatened your job. Not that you're the sort to murder someone."

I glared at her. She wasn't wrong, but it wasn't like I took Floyd particularly seriously. "He does that every time."

"The police don't know that," Olive pressed.

Mark rolled his eyes and started to turn away.

"It's too bad I didn't care to watch over him. I could have seen who did it," Olive said. She clapped her hands. "Then I'd just have had to lead the detectives to the killer. Of course, I could still do that but I have to figure out who actually murdered him."

"Did you notice the two wine glasses in his room?" I asked her.

Olive nodded. "He had to have had a visitor, but we don't know who. And it had to have been someone Floyd liked or else thought was important. That wasn't a cheap bottle of wine in there."

"He has me comp everything," I said making a face. "I have a special code so I know it was Floyd. If someone else in the family asks about the expenses, I let them know why. They can take it up with him."

Olive nodded. "A good idea. I just kept handwritten notes of the dates so that if I had to, I could refer back who was here. Of course, it meant going through my calendars over the months and if they asked more than a year later, I had to pull things out of storage. Fortunately, Ari knows that Floyd demands, er demanded, a lot so she made sure no one ever got too upset if it took me awhile to get the information."

"Do you think she'll be upset?" I asked. "About Floyd, I mean."

Olive stared down her nose at me. It's not as if she's much taller than I am, but Olive does do a good job of acting like it. I often wondered if she'd perfected that look in the mirror.

"Ari would probably dance a jig," Olive said drily. "Floyd was not her favorite brother. In fact, I'm not sure who he got on with, other than his mother. And from what I understand, she was even worse than he is, or er, was."

We all went silent for a moment.

"You don't think he'll end up haunting the hotel do you?" Suzanne asked, looking around as if expecting him to turn up.

Olive threw her hands up and disappeared.

"I don't think that was something Olive even wants to think about," Mark said. He chuckled a bit.

I had to admit, her reaction was amusing, though I couldn't say I was any more pleased at the thought of Floyd haunting the place than she was. I'd be stuck listening to him complain until I retired and left. If it happened, I'd probably retire in a few months though that would leave the hotel hanging. But there were some things I just could not imagine having to deal with. Floyd haunting the place was one of them. I wouldn't get my plans in place too quickly though. If I was unlucky enough to have added him to our haunts, perhaps he'd be one who couldn't speak. Then that could almost be fun.

It brought a slight smile to my face and as I turned to go back into my office. That was, of course, when the two detectives were just coming out of the elevator. I wiped the look from my lips, hoping they hadn't noticed, although given the way Detective Tinkerbell watched, I had a feeling she'd already seen. Just my luck. Here I was laughing because my boss was dead.

I kept going, in case they weren't coming down to talk to us. I took a picture of the information I had on the family and texted it to Detective Penn. He couldn't say I wasn't doing what he'd asked. I sighed.

At least Olive wasn't around to be questioned. While she could offer a lot of information, I had a feeling the police wouldn't be terribly accepting of the fact that she was dead. No doubt there'd be a huge investigation. I'd probably end up losing my job because who would believe in a ghost. I could only imagine the "logical" explanations they'd come up with, that would be anything but. No matter that I advertised the hotel as being haunted, I had a feeling most people chuckled at the conceit.

As suspected, the two detectives stopped at the desk and began asking questions. When Detective Penn got the information I'd sent, I heard his phone beep. That was a relief.

"We'll need a list of all the guests," Tinkerbell was saying.

"I'm sorry, the hotel attorneys have said we need a warrant for that," Mark said.

"You've already called your attorneys?" Tinkerbell demanded, as if that were a bad thing. We hadn't, but it was a standard answer we were told to give.

"Not to my knowledge," Mark said. "However, in the manager's handbook, that's the required answer. If you'd like to speak with our attorneys further about whether that's a rule we can break, I can offer you their number. I believe the firm is in Raleigh."

Actually, the firm was in New York, just like the

Bowmans, but they had offices in Raleigh. I pushed myself up and walked out.

"Can we be of assistance? Sometimes a specific request can be accommodated," I said. "I can, for instance, tell you the name of the guest who reported the smell. That's a normal part of working with local law enforcement."

"And her name would be?" Tinkerbell asked.

"Catalina Thomas," Mark read off the computer screen. He listed her room and the fact that she'd checked in two days ago and was leaving the next day.

"We'll need to speak with her first. Can you ring her room or do you need a warrant to do that?" Tinkerbell snapped.

Mark picked up the phone. I really didn't like this detective's attitude.

"How closely did you work with the deceased?" Tinkerbell asked me.

"Not terribly," I said. "The family normally allows me to run the hotel. Now and then they'll call and say one or more of them are coming to inspect the premises. I know they often send the attorneys in on visits to check over things they might miss. We might or might not be told about that. We usually get a warning for the family, though Floyd showed up unexpectedly yesterday."

I sometimes recognized the attorneys even if I wasn't told about the visit. If I didn't, Olive often did. Whoever got charged with checking on us generally spent a long weekend and enjoyed himself—rarely was it a woman—in the spa. I couldn't say how that was checking on us unless we failed some sort of customer service aspect. I suspected the Bowman's were just fine with that. It wasn't like anyone was embezzling from them. I kept a sharp eye on our books and we had an outside accounting firm who would report to me if there were problems with the finances.

I'd spotted the occasional problem in the restaurants and the managers there had quickly taken care of things. So far, I'd yet to hear from our accounting firm other than once when I'd just taken over. It wasn't Olive's fault. I just hadn't been trained and wasn't reporting in the proper style. That was quickly and easily remedied.

"They just trust you?" Tinkerbell looked surprised.

"We're monitored by an outside accounting firm and, as I said, the attorneys do spot checks," I reiterated. "The family has any number of holdings, so this isn't their bread and butter, so to speak. This was an old hotel that was inherited. I think a few of them thought a hotel would be fun to run and spent a great deal of money expanding and refurbishing it. They lost money for over two decades. I think they appreciate that we're running in the black, now."

Again, not Olive's fault. It had been a challenge to turn around. This part of the Appalachians wasn't exactly everyone's idea of the perfect getaway. And for those who wanted to come here, the spa wasn't the draw. When I'd started advertising this as a haunted hotel, that had begun to turn our fortunes around. I wasn't going to share that with the detectives, though.

I shouldn't need to. The local paper had covered the stories and why I thought that ghosts made good press. They could find out for themselves.

"You said that the victim just showed up this time without a warning?" Penn pressed.

"He did. That was unusual," I said. "I'm not sure it had ever happened before, at least not when I've worked here. I've been the manager for over twenty years and was employed here as the night manager for a few years before I became general manager."

Penn made a note. I noted a sidelong look over at

Tinkerbell, whose real name I still did not know. In the movies and books, the officers always identify themselves. At least I had a card for Penn.

"You said that the vic could be difficult?" Tinkerbell asked.

"He could."

"Was he difficult this time?"

"He wanted the Royal Suite which was already reserved for a honeymoon couple. I managed to persuade him to take the Owner's Suite. He wasn't happy about that. But I'm not sure there's much that does make Floyd happy."

Tinkerbell raised an eyebrow.

"You'll find that there aren't many people who know him who actually like him. I've heard rumors he's not popular with his siblings, either, though I can't confirm that." I was talking too much. Lyle had warned me against talking to much when the police came around.

Lyle Cook was a park ranger in the area. He often came to the assistance of the hotel when something went wrong. Thinking about him, I was surprised he hadn't come when we'd called 911. Even if he weren't the first on the scene, he normally checked in. While he could be frustrating, it did concern me that he wasn't around.

No one was acting normally lately. I had the ghost in room 785 that never showed up, showing himself. I had Olive wondering if she were a murderer. Floyd arrived unannounced. And now, Lyle was oddly unavailable.

"Interesting," Tinkerbell said. "Do you know of anyone who had an altercation with him when he arrived, besides yourself, of course?"

I disliked the insinuation. "I'm not sure we had an altercation. Floyd wanted something we could not give him. He did understand the type of publicity the hotel would get if we moved the honeymoon couple at the last minute so he accepted the change to the Owner's Suite. He hadn't bothered to book ahead. I just had to be firm with him."

Tinkerbell held my eyes, daring me to change my story. As if. I really did not like that woman.

I waited for her next question, wondering what that insinuation would be.

"Weren't you on duty during the storm when there was a murder at that time?" she asked.

"I was. Many of my staff were here, but the killer was found and arrested."

Tinkerbell nodded and made a note.

"You sent Ed the contact information for the siblings?"

I nodded.

"We'll be sure to chat with them to get their side of the relationship you had with Floyd," she said before leaving.

I watched her and Detective Penn walk out the door. She hadn't even bothered to give us a card if we wanted to contact her. For all I knew, she was someone Penn had hired to be the heavy.

When they left through the main doors, Suzanne blew out a breath.

"She's horrible. I can't believe her insinuation. As if just because Floyd was the owner and you work here, you're automatically under suspicion. I mean, if that's true, we're all under suspicion."

"Agreed," Mark said. "She didn't even ask if any of the rest of us knew if someone had had an altercation."

"I could have told her about the phone call," Suzanne said. "But she completely ignored me."

"I'm sure someone will be here to take information down," I said. "I was the person who called the police and waited near the body. I also knew Floyd."

Suzanne nodded, but continued to glare in the direction of the main doors. I couldn't help throwing my own glare in the direction the detectives had left. I could verbally defend Tinkerbell to my employee but that didn't mean I'd warmed to her questioning. I really did not like being a suspect.

Chapter Eight

Later that afternoon, when Suzanne and Mark had both had their lunches and I was just getting settled back into my work without having to force myself to concentrate over each little thing, Olive popped back in.

"I've been watching the crime scene investigators upstairs. It took them forever to move the body but they finally did and then others went over the entire room. The room is black and gray with their powders. I don't envy housekeeping. You'll need to have at least two people on that," she said.

"I've already ordered a new mattress," I said. "And called down to be sure we had extra linens."

Olive nodded. "Good. I popped into the closet and listened in. I've never so wished for a small closet with a door that closes. They weren't saying much. I did note that they took an interest in the wine glasses and the wine bottle. Someone was playing music in there. Madonna, I think. How awful is that?"

"I'm sure that music makes their work a bit less boring.

They do have to concentrate on all the little details and go over everything inch by inch," I said.

"I can't imagine writing about that in my novel. As they didn't say anything interesting, I did pop out again and watch. I'm sure I'll be able to incorporate that into my next book. Suzanne told you Floyd was arguing with someone as we were finishing last night?"

"She did," I said. "She didn't know who it was."

"Nor do I. I believe he was probably on his phone. He had quite a head of anger on him."

"I didn't say anything to the police, but I heard Jake arguing with him earlier that evening when I was heading to my apartment."

"Jake doesn't seem like a wine drinker," Olive said. "Of course, we're assuming that the guest was the one who murdered him. Floyd could have died later."

"The bottle of wine wasn't finished," I pointed out. I had a suspicion that Floyd would have finished it if he'd been given a chance.

"Perhaps the murderer interrupted him. The guest left and then Floyd was killed. Whoever he hosted could be in danger," Olive pointed out. "You have to find out who it was and who killed him. You don't need two murders in the hotel."

No, I really didn't. Tinkerbell seemed so interested in me that I couldn't help but think she'd already decided I did it.

"The woman detective was quite harsh in her questioning of me," I told Olive.

"She thinks you did it?" Olive was taken aback.

I nodded.

"Did you?" Olive asked. "I mean, not that I can judge. I probably killed that poor man in room 785."

"At worst you were a hit and run driver," I said.

"I could have hit him with the car on purpose," Olive said. "Or maybe I was just under the influence. That's still a crime. Did you have anything to drink last night? I've noticed you rarely imbibe, so you'd hardly have any ability to hold your alcohol. Perhaps Floyd asked you up there and you blacked it out?"

I smiled. "I'm actually quite certain I remember being home and searching for information on Corbin Moore. The cats can vouch for me."

"Well, at least I don't have to worry about Jake coming back to murder you then," Olive said. She frowned and glanced out the door. "Suzanne was with me. I popped out, though, and she had to pack up her computer. She could have done it."

"Why?" I asked.

Olive shrugged. "I'd say because Floyd was a shit, but he's not that much worse than so many other guests and she's never snapped. In fact, she's almost too easy going. I can't see how she'll make anything of herself."

I nodded at Olive to go on.

"The wine bothers me. I mean, I could see Jake doing something. I seem to recall when he first started he was attending anger management classes."

"He was," I said. "He'd been charged in an assault, but because he was otherwise an upstanding citizen, they sent him to the classes."

"Did he use a knife? It looked like a knife was used on Floyd."

"I think he might have picked up a knife in the fight or whatever," I said. "He said it was one of the stupidest things he ever did. He was mad and he was half drunk."

"He could have done it," Olive said.

"I'd hate to think so." I rubbed my hands across the thick wood on my desk. I breathed in the stink of cigarette smoke. I hated thinking that my head of security, someone who had saved my life not six months ago, could possibly be a murderer.

"I do, too," Olive said. "I didn't much like him when you hired him on, but he's grown on me."

My cell phone rang. I picked it up from its charging cradle on the edge of my desk and looked at it.

"Lyle?" I said. It was about time.

"I heard you had a murder in that hotel," he said. "I was taking care of some stuff. This time of year gets busy for me, but wanted to check in. The police got things taken care of?"

"They did. A Detective Penn and a woman who didn't introduce herself were there," I said.

"Penn's a good man if a bit lazy in his police work. Alice does the heavy lifting," Lyle said.

"Alice?" I pressed.

"Alice Granger," Lyle said. "She's sharp."

"She seems to be under the impression I did it," I said.

Lyle chuckled. "She's like that with everyone. At this point, unless she has a specific suspect, she probably has me on the list. Don't worry about it. I doubt she's even interviewed everyone she wants to. She'd talk to every guest in the hotel if she could, but I doubt you gave them a list."

"Can't," I said. Lyle knew about our policies. He'd been our acting police officer when we'd been snowed in and a guest had been killed earlier in the year. Lyle wasn't actually with the police but with the park service.

"She won't like that, but not much you can do. Later, she might set up a table and start talking to everyone."

"I'm surprised she left at all."

"Probably wanted to grab lunch. She'll be back, don't

worry. And if you get unlucky enough to listen in, you might find you got off easy."

Lyle warned me again about saying too much to the police, even if I did nothing. "We're trained to use that, you know."

With that he rang off. I set the phone down. Olive had popped out during the conversation. My stomach growled. I'd not eaten lunch, too upset by the questioning earlier, if not by finding Floyd's body, though that was rather stomach turning. The only reason I was able to be the least bit flip was because I disliked him so much.

A rather sad reflection on who I was. I sighed and got up, intending to go down to the café for one of their big salads. That would make a lovely lunch. I could get it to go and hide out in my apartment.

As I walked out to head down there, I noticed Detective Alice Granger walking back through the doors, looking intently at everything. Lyle was right. She did seem to look at everyone the same way she'd been staring at me. In fact, I wasn't certain but she might be thinking about whether the fireplace would have had means and motive.

Seeing Granger made me change my mind about lunch. Instead of heading downstairs I walked quickly down the hallway to the café. There was less chance of her seeing me that way. I felt badly about leaving Suzanne and Mark to the detective, but I'd spoken with her earlier. Hopefully, I'd be able to eat before having to do so again.

Chapter Nine

The café was at the end of the hall, behind the lobby bar. Instead of the dark tile and walls of the bar, it remained bright and airy with the light tile from the main lobby and bright cream walls. Small colorful images framed in white lined the walls. My favorite was of a basket of yarn balls, in all sorts of colors.

White tables with rounded chairs were scattered around the room. A hostess stood near a podium at the entrance. She led me to a table towards the back. I don't mind eating near the door to the kitchen because I know it's one of the less desirable tables. I'd trained my staff to be sure that anyone who worked there got the less desirable tables unless otherwise indicated, such as if they were there for a celebration.

I was pleased to note that most of the other tables were filled with diners. The hotel wasn't full, which often meant that the restaurants and bars weren't as busy as I'd like, but that appeared not to be true that afternoon. While I'd have liked the tables to all seat four or five people, even seeing two people there and the occasional singleton like myself was heartening.

The waiter was a young man I didn't know. His dark hair was thick and curled around his ears. He smiled easily and waved as I waited until he brought out salads to two women at a nearby table.

"Hey, what can I get you?" he asked.

"I'll have an iced tea and a Cobb salad," I said. "And a side of the bread you serve with the French onion soup."

He looked worried. "I don't know…"

"I'm Maggie. The hotel manager. If there's a problem, have your manager come talk to me." I gave him an encouraging smile, although it still made his hands shake slightly.

He looked eager to please and hurried away. I hoped he didn't forget my drink. The fact that I didn't recognize him did not mean he was a new employee, but in this case, I suspected it did. He wouldn't have been nearly so worried if he'd worked here for a time. We often hired local high school students in the summer. Their availability was usually around the times we were busiest.

I listened to the people around me talking. Their voices were low murmurs. A couple of women eating salads sat nearby.

"I wonder what's going on with the police," one of the salad women said to her friend. "Do you think there was a robbery or something?"

The other woman shrugged. "You know, I heard that a woman was murdered here earlier this year. Can you imagine? I hope we're not in her room. What if she's one of their famous ghosts?"

"I felt a cold spot in the lobby earlier. I was certain I was going to see something I didn't want to," the first woman said. I watched as she cut the lettuce in her salad into small pieces. She neglected to cut the too large portion of tomato and stuffed the entire thing along with some lettuce in her mouth getting dressing all over her lips. She daintily took a napkin and wiped, looking around as if hoping no one noticed.

I hurriedly looked away towards the back as if I were noticing something interesting back there.

Turning back towards the front, I noticed another woman walk in. I recognized Jean Marshall from when I checked her in the other day. She was dressed in a casual dress that floated around her slender figure. Her gray hair was sleek and almost damp at the ends. As I expected, she was one of our spa guests, though she liked to stay at haunted hotels whenever possible.

Seeing me, Jean smiled and gave me a wave. I recalled that she was from somewhere outside of Chicago. The Midwest folks were always so terribly friendly. I smiled and waved back.

After being seated Jean stood up and came over to me.

"I want to thank your entire staff for being so attentive and kind," she said. "I had a marvelous massage at the spa after my hike this morning. A perfect day."

"I'm glad you're enjoying yourself," I said.

"I am. It was a bit flustering to see a ghost. It wasn't at all what I was expecting, but he hasn't shown back up again. I would have loved to chat a bit more once I calmed down." Jean laughed at herself a little.

"Seeing he gave a name, I did some research. It seems that the ghost was a man killed in a car wreck later that day. Since so few people actually see him, I'm thinking he may only show up on the day he died." At least that was my theory. I could be wrong, but Jean might appreciate the fact that I was taking her knowledge seriously.

"I expect you're right. Ghosts do things like that. I find

them fascinating, even if I didn't expect to ever actually see one. And one that talked!"

Jean smiled again and gave me a small wave as she headed back to her table. Perhaps I should have invited to eat with me, but I wasn't sure I was up to making small talk with a guest.

My waiter came out followed by Gillian, the café manager.

"Hey Maggie," she said coming over with my ice tea. "You scared Mike to death with your order, but I got it taken care of. He's new this week."

"I thought I was perfectly nice."

"I think he's a little intimidated by authority figures," Gillian explained. She settled into the seat across from me and leaned over. In a loud hiss she whispered, "I heard Floyd got himself topped."

She raised her eyebrows to ask the question.

"You heard right," I said.

Gillian nodded. "Do you know where Ryan was?"

"Ryan?" I asked.

"Ryan Phillips up in the Mezzanine Bar?" Gillian said.

"No?" I sipped my ice tea, enjoying the slightly bitter taste. While we make a very fine sweet tea, or so I'm told, I'm not enough of a Southerner to have tried it.

"He and Floyd did not get on at all."

Now it was my turn to lean forward. "I hadn't heard."

I looked around. No one had noticed that we were whispering like a pair of school girls. The conversation continued to hum around us, with people eating their food. One of the waitresses brought out a plate that included fries, which smelled heavenly and made me wonder if I'd chosen correctly when I'd ordered my salad.

Gillian nodded. "About a year ago, when Floyd was here for his annual inspection as he calls it…"

I raised an eyebrow cutting Gillian off. "I've never heard the term."

"He probably knows you'd snap right back at him," Gillian said.

I smiled, thinking that I'd at least slightly cowed Floyd. Good to know I had it in me.

"At any rate, during that time, he started in on Ryan who told him he ought to go, well, you know…"

I nodded. I could imagine Ryan's language. It wasn't the sort of thing I often said, but I knew that others were not quite so fastidious. Perhaps it made me a fussy old lady, but if it did, then perhaps I was.

"Well, Floyd responded that at least he wasn't watering drinks and saving the extra for himself and basically said that even that was theft and he could make sure Ryan got caught. Ryan's face turned ten shades of red and he looked like he was going to dive over the bar and throttle Floyd. Floyd backed up and laughed and said not to worry, his secret was safe."

"Really?" I asked. I hadn't ever noticed that the mezzanine bar went through alcohol faster than they should. Of course, if Ryan were covering his tracks by adding water to other drinks or even the bottles themselves, then I probably wouldn't notice. I'd have to have an auditor look into that, but it would be a pain.

"Really," Gillian said.

"I've never noticed anything off about the bar, nor have I gotten complaints."

"It was probably just Floyd making something up, but it would be a tough one to prove and could get Ryan in a lot of trouble with a different manager," Gillian said.

"I wish he would have said something to me. Of course, that was last year."

"Ryan said that Floyd would regret that accusation.

When Floyd laughed, Ryan told him to wait. He was smart enough to know his revenge would be better if it wasn't expected or something like that."

I sighed. Ryan often shared wine tips with people. While Floyd was probably talking about the hard liquor which would be easier to water, Ryan could easily have been the one drinking wine with Floyd. It seemed like a flimsy reason to kill someone.

Mike came back with my salad and bread. Gillian nodded to me and left. I wondered if Detective Granger would get to the café to interview her and whether she'd share Ryan's altercation. Even if she did, would the detective give it any more credence than I did? A year was a long time to hold a grudge.

Chapter Ten

Back in my office, I had a hard time concentrating. There were two people on my staff who had potential reasons to want Floyd dead. I didn't want it to be someone I knew. I didn't know Ryan well, but he was someone I had agreed to hire. I wondered if the altercation Gillian had told me about really was just about watering drinks.

Watering drinks wasn't a horrible thing. Ryan drinking the alcohol that he supposedly served was an issue. That was theft. Of course, as I'd pointed out, it would be impossible to prove. If Ryan had come to me, it wouldn't be an issue. In fact, I would have figured that Floyd had expected a stronger drink. Ryan had perhaps made it normally and Floyd was pissed. It was the sort of thing Floyd would get upset about.

What concerned me was Ryan's reaction. I mean, if he wanted to take care of it himself there were many reactions, but he'd gotten mad. I guess if I were proud of what I did and I did it by the book, I might have been angry about the accusation, but would it be a strong enough reaction that it appeared I wanted to strangle someone? That seemed over the top. Of course, this was all third hand tales.

I had second hand information of a heated phone call by Floyd from Suzanne. I didn't know who he'd been talking to, but that person could have had a reason to kill him. And then there was Jake. I'd heard that altercation. But I really didn't want it to be Jake. I ought to go talk to him to find out what was what.

I stood up and went out to the front. Suzanne and Mark were busily working on checking in a couple of people who had just arrived. It was getting to be that time.

"I'll be downstairs," I said leaving. I'd have my cell phone.

I left and went down to the employee elevator. I normally take the stairs whenever I can but the elevator was easier down to the sub-basement. I wouldn't have to walk down the hallway towards my apartment, which was good exercise, nor would I have to go down the cement staircase that led to the subbasement. I always felt as if I were on my way to a bunker when I did that.

The subbasement wasn't a bad place once you were there, but the stairwell needed brightening. It was on a long list of things I'd like to do but it had never quite passed the test of whether it was worth my time to write up a proposal for it. Part of the reason was that I wasn't sure how it would make the hotel function better. It wasn't as if I had employees complaining about it.

The security office was right next to the stairwell, a short walk down the subbasement hallway from the elevator. The hall might not have windows but it was carpeted and looked like much of the rest of the hotel, although this area tended to smell like a dormitory filled with old socks and empty pizza boxes. The latter were probably actually sitting on a desk in the warren of offices.

The main door was solid wood. One of the guards sat at the front desk and looked up when I entered. He was playing a game on his phone, though he didn't have any earbuds in. I didn't mind. The desk person was there as a sort of receptionist for the office, making sure they knew who was in and if not, where they were. They took phone calls and routed people towards any trouble spots.

The team rotated through watching the security cameras, walking the hotel, and sitting at the front desk. It was the best way to keep people focused when they were monitoring the cameras.

"Is Jake in?" I asked.

"Down in his office," the young man said. I noticed his shirt said his name was Gunnar.

"Thanks, Gunnar," I said.

He looked surprised that I knew his name, probably having forgotten that with the yellow vest he wore, he had a name badge on. Gunnar appeared about to say something else but then turned back to his computer as if he had work to do, though I knew he didn't.

I walked down the hallway, noticing which of the guards were clearly paying attention to their monitors and which were a bit more lax. It wasn't an exciting job so I was pleased that most were being fairly attentive. If something did happen, we'd have it recorded, but I'd rather be proactive about an incident than have to look it up later.

Jake was in his office sure enough, but with him was Detective Penn, the man's large frame filling the small office, really not much bigger than my closet.

"Maggie?" Jake said.

"I was going to make sure all was going okay down here," I said, not sure what to say. I'd been at lunch and if the detectives had had any sort of warrant for our security footage, there would have been no reason to contact me. Jake would handle that anyway.

"Your head of security was showing me the footage from last night," Penn said.

"They didn't have a warrant, yet," Jake apologized. "I hope that won't get us in trouble. But he just asked to see the footage from that hallway."

It was probably fine.

"I can't let you take it without a warrant but we won't mention that you were here earlier," I said. "It's not as if the guests have a particular expectation of privacy on a hallway with a visible camera."

At least that was something I had heard. I didn't know if it were true or not. I really needed to sit down with our attorney and go over how far we could go in being helpful with the police. It wasn't as if the hotel was crime-ridden but it did seem as if we'd been seeing a bit more than our fair share of police lately.

"Exactly what I said," Jake told me. He went back to watching the video. I leaned around Penn so I could see the screen as well. Not much was happening just then. I noted the time stamp was only seven.

"I think Suzanne said she'd heard Floyd on the phone with someone around eight," I reported.

"And you didn't tell us?" Penn asked.

"No one asked me. Besides, I figured you and your partner or someone would talk directly to her. She's the one who heard it. I have no way of judging whether or not she was certain it was Floyd." I glared at Penn.

Penn nodded, but made a note.

"Let's fast forward this for a bit. We might see him leave the room." Penn sat up watching the quickly moving video intently.

We didn't see Floyd leave, but around eight, Jake slowed it back down, though it was still fast. We saw Floyd return about quarter past eight. Around eight-thirty someone delivered a cart with wine and glasses. I thought there might be a plate of chocolates of the sort that we served in the restaurant that adjoined the hotel. Those weren't normally on the room service menu, but I'm sure Floyd pitched a fit.

The employee, who I didn't recognize, quickly pushed the cart inside and then left.

About fifteen minutes later the feed became staticky, and then went to fog. Jake used the fast forward through about an hour, when the camera came back online.

"We might have had a power glitch," he said, though I heard the uncertainty in his voice.

"Convenient," Penn said, echoing my thoughts. "Who would have access to the cameras?"

"Anyone in security," Jake said. "Maggie might, not that she'd know what to do."

Penn looked at me, probably to see if I took offense to the comment. I just smiled and shrugged. I left the computer stuff to my employees. I could use email and my work programs and I was getting good at doing internet searches, but I was far from an expert.

"Anyone not on the security staff would probably have been noticed down here," Jake said, "But it might be possible to hack into the system if they were on another hotel terminal somewhere, so really any employee with sufficient computer savvy could have done it. And, of course, no firewall is one hundred percent effective. We had an outside company set up our firewalls, plus I have a very competent employee who maintains them, but it could be possible. Just not easy. You'd need some very specialized knowledge."

"Please don't tell me there's an IT conference on site," Penn said, frowning.

I shook my head. "That's not something we've had here before," I said. "Fortunately. We mostly get ghost hunters."

"So I heard," Penn replied easily. Then he sighed. "We'll be back with the warrant. I know you'll be tempted to see what you can find out about that glitch, but leave it. I want our people to have a go at it, or rather the state's people, before anyone messes with it again."

Jake nodded.

Penn stood up and brushed his shirt over his abdomen. He nodded at both of us, stepped around me, and left. He'd been slightly sweaty and I got a good strong whiff of the delightful gym sock scent that permeated the place. I wondered if I'd stink like socks when I left as well.

"What do you think?" Jake asked.

I glanced down the hallway, to make sure Penn was still weaving through the maze. I listened to him say something to Gunnar at the front desk before speaking again.

"I don't know," I finally said. "I did, however, hear you and Floyd arguing about something earlier in the evening. I haven't said anything about it, but I wanted to chat with you in case I get asked more directly."

Jake sighed and ran his hands through his hair.

"Floyd gets to me. I mean he's the sort who's always pushing. He wanted to see some footage of the lobby shortly before he arrived. He said he thought he recognized someone in there. but wanted to be certain before talking to them."

I raised an eyebrow.

"I know, right?" Jake said. "We had a bit of an argument. I mean, he is the owner. I suppose technically he has a right, but I wanted to run it by the attorneys. Floyd was pissed. That ticked me off. I like this job."

"You sounded a bit more heated than that," I said. And the way Jake talked, it seemed like there was more to the story, but I wasn't sure how to ask or if he'd tell me if I did ask.

Jake made a face. "You know Floyd."

I did know Floyd. Even if Jake didn't have anger management issues in his past, Floyd could have made someone willing to jump down his throat.

"I had to ask," I said. "Did you mention this to Penn when he was here?"

Jake reddened. "I didn't really want to get into it. I mean I thought I might be one of the last people to see him and I don't need the police digging up my background."

"No, you don't," I said. "But it would have been better if you'd owned up talking to him before they dig it up anyway. I mean, if they can't find a particular suspect, they'll look at all of us. I swear, Detective Granger wants to pin this on me."

Jake laughed at that, easing the tension in his face. He was hiding something. I just didn't know what. My stomach clenched at the thought that it might be the fact that he'd been the one to murder Floyd.

Chapter Eleven

When I got back to the desk, Mark mentioned that Detective Granger had interviewed both he and Suzanne. I hoped that Suzanne had been forthcoming about hearing Floyd, particularly since I'd mentioned it. I completely forgot that we might have to mention Olive was there. Of course, I suppose Suzanne could say she was working on a book for a friend and wouldn't get distracted down in the conference room.

I looked around at the lobby. There were plenty of people around but fortunately, I had a couple of part-time workers dealing with the desk. Coming up on the weekend, we always got busier. I decided to head back to the office to try and get some actual work done.

The chair in there felt too hard on my behind. My feet ached slightly. I sighed, wondering what the weather was like. I often got achy and restless before a storm. That was just what we didn't need. It was a bit early for thunderstorms, but it had been unseasonably warm lately.

I finally settled in and started staring at my computer, my head slightly raised so that I could look through the lower part of my bifocals. I'd hated having to get them and I tried not to think about them. It was my one vanity about aging, having to admit that I could no longer see close up well enough without my glasses.

Just as I got comfortable and into the swing, Olive popped in.

"Did you learn anything new?" she asked.

"Detective Penn was downstairs in the security office and we found that someone made the camera in the hallway outside Floyd's room glitch for nearly an hour last night, probably about the time he was murdered," I said.

Olive frowned. "I was actually asking about Corbin Moore. I want to know if I was the one who hit him with my car."

"I'm not sure how I can find that out," I said. "If there was anything on film, they would have found it then."

Olive sighed. "I don't suppose Office Amsden still works there? Or even lives around here? You could probably call him. I remember working with him several times."

I went to the internet and started looking up our local police officers. No one named Amsden. I mentioned that to Olive.

I racked my brain to try and figure out who might have been around. I recalled reading something about Brandon's father, but he wouldn't be helpful as he had dementia. Even so, I told Olive.

"If only he could remember," she said. "Can you think of anyone who might be around? I know Lyle started here around the same time you did. Almost as if you were meant to know each other."

I glared at Olive. She'd gotten this idea that Lyle and I should be a couple. Fortunately, the only person she seemed to have mentioned this to was me, so I didn't have to fend off any other matchmakers. While I liked Lyle just fine, I couldn't picture us as anything more than friends.

Quite honestly, I liked my little apartment and had no desire to move off-site. I couldn't believe Lyle would want to move in there, nor would there be much room for him. I mentally berated myself for even imagining the two of us in a more serious relationship than either of us might want. For all I knew, Lyle had no interest in me, and even if he did, who knew if we'd want to live together? We were both very independent.

This was why I quite liked my own company. I knew myself. I didn't have to worry about what another person was thinking nor did I have to attempt to please anyone else. Just me.

Even the cats occasionally threw me when one of them decided to do something out of character. I'd worry that they were dying and would rush them to the vet, often to find out there was nothing wrong and they were in the peek of good health. Once, Chai had had a slight bit of nasal congestion and they gave me some medication, mostly to make sure it didn't develop into something worse and to make sure he kept eating.

I'd been a mess, at least internally. However, I'd kept it together for my workers.

Since starting self-defense and then jiu jitsu, I had begun talking to Dori at the martial arts class. I'd been attempting to work on my anti-social side a bit more, though I hadn't exactly told anyone this. That was just a bridge too far. I'd been self-sufficient for far too long. But perhaps if one of the cats got sick again, I'd be able to admit that I was concerned. That sounded appropriately neutral and yet conveyed so much.

"I think you need to call Lyle and ask him," Olive said. Or rather I should say she demanded.

Knowing she wasn't going to let this go, I picked up the phone and called Lyle. He answered on the first ring. He must have been holding his phone, perhaps looking something up.

"Maggie. What is it?"

"Olive is here and she has a question," I said.

"Oh?" Lyle knew about Olive. He was fairly comfortable with her, though that wasn't true of all our ghosts. Still, he knew she'd been instrumental in helping to save my life earlier in the year. She'd distracted the killer long enough for him and Jake to come rescue me.

"We found the ghost in room 785. Apparently, he only shows up on the day he died. And he was killed in a car wreck." I paused to collect what I wanted to say and to verify the year Corbin died. "Anyway, he recognized Olive and she's worried she might have been involved in his accident. She can't recall. Is there anything you remember about that car wreck?" I went on to explain a bit more and added in the year, hoping the details might jog a memory, though I knew in my case, that wouldn't be true, not unless I'd been there to see it.

While Lyle wasn't on the police force, as the park ranger in the area, he often knew details about crimes that were committed locally.

"That was a long time ago," Lyle said. "It was the first time I'd gotten stationed here and I was only around for perhaps a year. If nothing came out right around that time, I wouldn't know about."

"Do you remember anything?" I pressed.

"I'll have to go back through some of my journals and look up a few things online. Maybe that will jog my memory. You'd think that when I came back and heard that Olive had died that I'd have felt something if I thought she was a murderer. Like, 'Oh good, I don't have to worry about being murdered now.'"

I chuckled.

Olive glared at the phone in my hand. Fortunately, we were not on a video call so Lyle couldn't see her. He'd probably rethink the whole not being murdered thing. She appeared to sit on the edge of my desk as she continued glaring.

Still, Lyle and I chatted a bit more. He asked about the investigation into Floyd's murder. My other phone rang and I told him I had to go.

I was a popular woman that day. I should have figured I would be, given that there'd been a death. That's the sort of upset that throws everyone off and, of course, everyone wants to discuss it.

I picked up the phone. It was Ari Bowman. My mouth went dry as I tried to think of something appropriate to say.

Chapter Twelve

Olive raised an eyebrow at me from her position near the edge of the desk. If I had a smaller desk, she would have seemed as if she were hovering over me. But this thing was huge. I could have laid down on it with my head at one end and had plenty of room for my computer at the other. Of course, doing so would have forced me to breathe in the decades of second-hand smoke that had leached into the wood.

We'd refinished the desk, but I wondered if we used some of that sealant if that would seal in the smell. It was something to file away for a more appropriate time.

"I don't know what to say," I told Ari.

Ari's voice had that scratchy sound that older women who smoked for years tend to have. So far as I knew, Ari had given up the habit. She'd spent a week at the spa about a decade ago trying to kick it. While she said she was horrible during her visit, I and the entire staff preferred her at her worst to Floyd at his usual.

"Hallelujah wouldn't be inappropriate," Ari said. Then

she sighed. "It is a shock though. And I'm surprised at how empty I feel."

I made appropriate noises, at least I hoped so. Olive was leaning over the desk now, to listen to the phone call more closely. I was on the office phone, which was an old black thing that I held up to my ear. Olive couldn't hear the other person as easily as she could when I was on my cell phone. I shivered with the cold that she brought with her.

"It was certainly a shock here," I said.

"It's troubling that he was murdered. Did you recognize anyone who was there?" she asked. "I'm sure Floyd never endeared himself to anyone, really, except that little gold-digger who finally couldn't stand him any longer. I'd have expected she would have murdered him."

"I didn't recognize anyone, but if he's got an angry ex, perhaps a name?" I fumbled around in the center drawer of the desk for a pen and a pad of paper, ready to write.

"Kate Bowman, unless she eventually decided to give up the name, then she'd be Kate Thompson."

I made a note. Then I clicked on our system to check out names of our guests. A few clicks and I was in.

"I'm checking out records, just to be certain. I know you're not legal, but we'll be getting requests for a list of our guests. Jake already showed one of the detectives the security footage for the hallway near Floyd's room, but we want a warrant to give them a copy and for other areas."

"Did Jake tell you anything about what the footage showed?" Ari asked.

"Nothing. I was there. It seems like the camera had a glitch for about an hour."

"Someone planned this. Can one of your security people track who, when, and where it might have happened?"

"The detective wants us to avoid doing that. He'll have someone from the state's crime lab do it."

Ari sighed. "I suppose that's best. Do the police have any suspects?"

"There's a detective here who seems to suspect everyone. The guest next to Floyd called down to complain about a smell. Maintenance followed his nose to Floyd's room and asked if he should enter. He got no response to a knock. When he found Floyd, he called me and I called the police when I got up there. The detective on the case questioned me quite harshly as if I had set this whole thing up," I explained, a little aggrieved.

"We could be twin murderers, then," Olive said. "At least I didn't get caught."

"Is there someone there?" Ari asked.

"It's just Olive," I said.

"She's still there?" Ari asked.

It says something about Ari that she could so casually mention a ghost as if Olive were still a breathing human she often saw at the hotel.

"She's writing a book," I said.

Ari laughed. "A ghost writer, huh?"

I chuckled at her pun.

"I shouldn't laugh," she said. "I'm sure everyone will think I'm a horrid woman. Keep me posted. If you need any extra legal assistance, I'll make sure you get it. My goal is to find out who killed Floyd. I'm not sure if it's for justice or to reward them, but I'll figure it out."

Ari hung up without the usual niceties. All the Bowmans were like that. They were used to people jumping to do their bidding.

Olive fingered her pearls. "I can see there was no love lost between the two of them. I mean, I knew that, but Ari was…"

"I think she might have had a couple already," I said, glancing at the clock. Ari's voice had been smoother and her pun was unlike the woman I normally spoke with.

"Oh definitely," Olive said. "Ari never starts before noon and rarely ends before midnight. It's why she knew exactly where to send me to dry out after my divorce."

There were certain things I didn't want to know about my employer. It didn't change who Ari was, of course, and she wasn't directly involved in any of the running of the hotel. The Bowmans had people for that. It was only when, as owners, they were being asked to spend money that they had to sign off on things. And well, they were all intrigued by the thought of owning a haunted hotel.

I suppose if I had inherited a haunted hotel among my other assets, I'd find that intriguing as well.

"Oh dear," Olive said looking up. "There's that detective again."

And with that, she stepped around my desk and popped out. I hoped the Detective hadn't noticed her and demanded whoever else was in the office come out to be questioned.

Chapter Thirteen

I wasn't surprised when one of my desk workers poked their head into the office and said that the detective wanted to speak with me. I stood up and went out front. The lobby bar was in full swing. Jazz music from upstairs battled lightly with the pop music from the lobby area. The people in the bars never seemed annoyed, but I always found it slightly irritating.

Suzanne had clearly headed off, but Mark was still there with the afternoon workers checking in a few more people. The woman standing next to the detective must have bathed in a sort of floral perfume. I hoped I didn't start sneezing.

"Do you want to go in my office?" I asked pleasantly. I wasn't sure I wanted Detective Granger in my office, but I also didn't want to talk about a dead man at the front desk.

"Fine." Granger made it sound like I'd insisted she take a two hour hike when she was ready for a bed and a bath. I opened the door that led behind the desk. Then I ushered her into my office.

I noted her looking around. For once, having another

person in there didn't make the place feel too small. She grabbed one of the chairs off to the side of the desk. I settled in the office chair which was so used to me, it rather conformed to my behind. Not comfortably, of course, but at least I was used to the hardness.

"What can I help you with?" I asked.

"I talked to the Bowmans," she said. "None of them seemed particularly upset."

"It can be difficult to tell over the phone," I said.

"You mentioned only Floyd was here?" Granger pressed, ignoring my comment. So much for helping Ari.

"Yes."

"Arianna Bowman's phone pings to this area," Granger replied. "Are you sure she isn't here?"

"I looked up something on the computer recently and her name wasn't on the guest list," I said. I hoped that was okay. What was Ari playing at? She could have told me she was in the area. I wouldn't have been insulted if she decided to stay at one of the B&Bs or the Comfort Inn over in Boone.

"I assume you'd recognize her?" Granger asked.

"I would. I'm not sure who else would. Both managers have been here long enough that they've probably met her…" I couldn't verify it though. Usually if Ari showed up, I checked her in. It was just easier to make sure she got everything she needed and I could make sure there weren't any issues with billing. The owners, of course, got their stays comped.

Granger made a note.

"Are you sure she's here?" I asked.

"Just that her phone is up in this area," Granger said. "When we originally called, her office was cagey about where she was so I had someone ping her phone."

I wondered how legal that was, but I wasn't about to go

lecturing a detective, particularly not this detective. I just plastered a pleasant look on my face and waited.

"We've also not been able to get a hold of this Catalina Thomas. Do you know where she could be?"

"Our guests don't normally check in with us. She reported the smell. We sent someone up, but she didn't say if she'd be out and about or in her room. We are a hotel. People aren't normally here just to enjoy the facilities. They also want to hike or visit friends or whatever."

I hadn't checked her in, so I had no idea what type Catalina might be.

"Have you checked with our spa services? They might know if she was on the books."

"They checked. She wasn't," Granger replied shortly. "I'll need you to contact me when she returns."

"Guests don't report in," I said. "They often by-pass the desk and just go to their room. Besides, I'll be off at five or so…"

Although I rarely actually made it back downstairs at that time, in theory that was when I got off work. I loved my job and didn't mind that there was often something else to do or tidy or check on when others would have been relaxing. It kept me busy and feeling useful.

"You could have the other desk workers watch for her," Granger said.

"I'm not even sure what she looks like. I didn't check her in," I said. "This is a hotel, not a Bed and Breakfast where the owner knows all the guests and can hear them in their rooms. I can ask security to look and see if someone goes into her room, but that doesn't mean they'll see someone do so."

Granger made a note. She sighed as if I were being particularly difficult.

"That will have to do."

I made a note to myself to call down and talk to Jake. He'd have his people on it. I wasn't sure if this was something legal or not.

"I saw someone else in your office a few minutes ago," Granger said. "Who was that?"

"Oh, that was just Olive. She worked here." I hoped Granger didn't ask more than that.

She made a note.

"Was she around yesterday?"

"Olive is always sort of around," I said. I felt myself starting to sweat. I hoped that the Detective didn't take that as a sign of guilt.

"Could she have seen something?"

"If she did, she'd have mentioned it by now. She likes to let me know all the details of what she's noticed." If Olive weren't a ghost, that would probably be weird. I did not, however, know how Detective Granger would take learning that the woman she'd seen in here was one of our ghosts. While those who worked at the hotel often got used to the idea, most people were freaked out by it.

My forehead itched where the sweat was beading. I could only hope that Officer Granger didn't notice.

Instead of pressing me, she just made a note. Chances were, she'd be asking people about Olive. I couldn't warn the entire hotel staff so I had no idea what they'd say or how the detective would take it. Would she assume I had a friend named Olive as well as there being a ghost? Would she think I was deliberately lying to her? I had no idea. I suppose Ari would stand up for me, but if she were a suspect, we might end up having to defend ourselves together against the charges.

Finally, the questioning stopped and Granger left me alone. I breathed out a deep sigh as soon as she was gone. Then I gave myself some welcome relief from the itchiness of my forehead and came away with damp fingers. There was no way the detective didn't know I was sweating. Perhaps I could pass it off as a hot flash.

I bit my lip. Granger had been much nicer to me this time. The first time she'd been like a dog with a bone trying to get me to admit to anything. Either she'd found an alibi for me somewhere or else she was, as the old saying went, trying catch more flies with honey. And, unfortunately, I was the fly.

Olive popped back in. She'd probably been watching the whole time.

"What did she want?"

I told her about Ari.

"Interesting," Olive said. "I had no idea. And Ari didn't tell you?"

I shook my head.

"I can't imagine where she'd stay if she wasn't staying here. And her name wasn't in the computer?" Olive pointed at my screen, as if that was the computer.

"Nope. Do you really think she could have come here under a false name. She'd have to make sure she came in when I wasn't here," I said.

"Easy enough to do a late check-in and hope," Olive said. "Or maybe if she saw you through the doors, she could have called and had someone lure you away. If she did murder Floyd, something I wouldn't blame her for at all, she could have just walked in after staying somewhere else."

"There are some nice Bed and Breakfasts around," I said.

Olive nodded, looking thoughtful.

"What are you thinking?" I asked.

"Nothing," Olive said. "I was trying to think if I'd seen her on the property at all and I can't say I recall. Not that I watch all the time. Sometimes I just turn off, so to speak. It's rather like that when I'm not around."

I didn't want to inquire too deeply what it was like to be a spirit. I mean, all of them had different rules. Perhaps some were trapped having to watch everything around them or reflect upon their earthly lives.

"I think Granger saw you in my office. She asked who was here. I gave your name. She wanted to know if you were around yesterday. I said you were always sort of around and that you used to work here. I have no idea what she'll ask other people about. She was much nicer this time, which I don't like," I said.

"Do you think she was playing good cop in an attempt to win you over so you confessed?" Olive asked.

"If I had anything to confess to, perhaps." I glared at Olive.

She smiled her superior smile at me. Then it faded and she became pensive again.

"I wish Lyle would hurry up with information about that car accident. I want to know if I may have accidentally-on-purpose murdered someone and got away with it. Can you imagine? Me? A murderess?"

"I find it rather alarming that you're so excited about it," I said.

"Only because if I was, I got away with it. You know how many murderers are caught? Particularly those who kill on the spur of the moment?"

Olive went on to give me statistics which she'd probably picked up from Suzanne. Which reminded me that my desk worker was probably down in the conference room with her dinner, working away.

"Don't you have to meet with your editor today?" I asked.

Olive humphed. "I should. But she was just eating

dinner when I debated joining her. And really, I wanted to find out what the detective knew. I want to congratulate Floyd's killer before they're taken away. Even if it wasn't you."

With that Olive disappeared, giving me the sort of look my mother gave me when she was disappointed in me. I almost felt guilty for not having murdered Floyd myself. But then I shook that off and settled myself in to do some of the work that hadn't gotten done earlier in the day.

Chapter Fourteen

I managed to get quite a bit of work done without any interruptions. I greeted Addy, my night manager with a wave, and then nodded at Mark when he left. I should have talked to him and to Suzanne about what the detective had asked them while she was there, but I was feeling guilty enough about not doing as much work as I should have.

It's not as if a murder happened in the hotel every day. I could easily finish my work some other time, but I wanted to get a few of my tasks done, almost as if I felt I was going on vacation. Perhaps my subconscious was worried I'd be put in jail.

The smell of pizza began to overwhelm the front desk area and I pushed myself up. Jimmy Buffet was singing about changes in the lobby bar and I found myself wanting to step to the music. The mountains had always been my home, whether in the west or, now, here in the Appalachians, but I did have a soft spot for him.

"How's it going?" I asked Addy.

Addy was in her late twenties and just getting started

on her hotel management career. She wasn't certain she wanted to stay in the hospitality industry but she was comfortable at the Neary-Ten and I was happy to help her explore her career options. She had a good head for business and was very reliable. I figured she'd go far in whatever career she decided to hop over to, even if it was just leaving our little resort for something larger and more glamourous. She really was wasted as a night manager.

Mark, however, was local and he was unlikely to leave his post any time soon. I'd be sorry to have either of them leave.

"I heard Floyd was murdered last night," Addy said, looking at me, her eyes large. "And there's a detective wandering around questioning everyone."

"Even the guests?" I asked.

"I think it's mostly the employees. She's been looking for a guest named Catalina, though. Mark said he called up to that room a few times but there's been no answer."

"She asked me about her," I said. "Catalina called down to complain about a smell."

"Wow," Addy said. "Floyd came down and demanded I do something about the loud music in the lobby bar last night."

"What time?" I asked.

"About seven-thirty, I think," Addy said.

Before he was arguing with someone on the phone then. I filed that away.

"Have you talked to the detective yet?"

Addy shook her head. "She hasn't been back here. Probably is still talking to the evening shift workers in the restaurant and bars."

Which would make sense. If Floyd had been out and about, perhaps one of them had seen him or dealt with him.

I tapped my fingers on the wood of the desk.

"If Catalina comes back, she is allowed in her room, isn't she? It's not a crime scene?" Addy asked.

"Floyd was killed in his room so I think the detective just wants to ask her what she noticed."

"I'll let Catalina know if she has questions. The crime scene van was still outside when I came in so they're probably around. There was a patrol car out front as well. She'll probably notice what's going on and have questions

"If she wants us to move her room, we can. No charge. Upgrade her if we have a suite."

"Oh! Last night someone told me that the woman in 785 saw the ghost?" Addy brightened.

"She did. The ghost's name is Corbin Moore. I guess he died in a car accident on the day he appeared. It might be that he only appears on that day. It'll be something to add to the website soon."

I ought to do that. I put it off so that I could make sure Olive had nothing to do with the murder. While it would be something salacious for our followers if the former manager had murdered someone with her car, I didn't want rumors about Olive to start if there was nothing to it. Not that she seemed particularly unhappy about the possibility of being a murderer.

I guess I could see her point. It wasn't as if they could do anything to her now for murdering the guy.

Addy and I talked about a few other stray things going on around the hotel. She made a note for herself on Catalina Thomas's booking. It occurred to me that Catalina Thomas was quite similar to the name Kate Thompson, who was supposedly Floyd's prior wife.

Instead of heading down to my apartment I went back to my office and did a quick search on Catalina Thomas. My cats would probably be annoyed with me for making them wait for dinner. I found the driver's license number Catalina had left us for our records, so I had a state to limit my searches for her name. Of course, it was North Carolina so it could have been a rental car.

Not finding much, I sighed. It could have been so easy. The similarity in names seemed too coincidental. I decided it might be worth heading up to the top floor and checking to see how the police were getting on. Perhaps they had someone stationed outside Catalina's room.

There was a short wait for the elevator and it discharged three lovely young women all laughing and talking. They were in casual colorful jeans and knit shirts filled with sparkles and sequins. A blonde with long hair still had slightly damp ends. I suspected they'd been here for the spa. Probably a girl's weekend.

Stepping in, I felt someone hurrying in behind me. I turned. Jean. She looked more put together than she had when she'd seen the ghost or even at lunch.

"What's going on?" she asked as the doors closed. She pressed the floor for seven. I went to the top floor.

"Not a whole lot," I told her. I mean there was, but I wasn't going to discuss it with a guest.

"There's a detective talking to all your employees. Are you having a problem?"

"Not really," I said. "A guest passed away last night and she's making sure they cross all their T's and dot their I's."

I suppose that was close enough.

"Really? It seems so strange to think of someone dying here. Of course, there's a ghost in my room. But it seemed like he died in a car wreck," Jean said thoughtfully. "That's so interesting. You know I looked him up."

"Really?" Maybe she knew something. It seemed like she was eager to chat, perhaps too eager. I suspected she might be lonely here by herself.

"The memorials were all very nice but I found some comments from prior to his death. He wasn't well-liked at his work place. It's the sort of thing that gets picked up as employers scanned HR records. He got fired from two different jobs. He was some sort of manager in banking. But, by the time he was killed he'd moved to being a manager of a chain of payday type lenders. Supposedly higher end than those commercial stores around."

"How interesting," I said. She seemed to have better information than I did. I'd have to tell Olive.

"He was in a car wreck. You have to wonder if he'd just decided to end it all given that he was kind of losing credibility in his industry. They said he wasn't drinking in the reports, but who knows? I mean it was a one car accident. It had to be one or the other. Either that or a very creative murder."

The elevator doors opened onto the seventh floor. Jean stepped out.

"It was nice chatting with you," she gave me a wave.

I waved back. While I hadn't exactly wanted to chat with her, at least she was nice. And she gave me something else to share with Olive. She did seem a bit excited to impart the information, but then again, I was always excited to learn things about the ghosts here so I couldn't fault her.

The elevator continued up to the top floor and I exited. Soft music played in the background and if I weren't looking for a police presence I might not have noticed. An officer stood leaning against the wall across from the owner's suite while the crime scene crew continued their work. I supposed they had to go through everything in the hotel room. Not a job I'd relish.

"I'm sorry…" he started.

I paused and held up a hand.

"I'm Maggie Davenport and I'm the manager. I was just checking to see if you'd had any problems." There, that gave me a reason to be there.

"No ma'am. I'm sure someone would have contacted you if they had."

"Have the guests in the rooms behind you had any complaints?" It was certainly possible that they'd said something to the officers on duty, but not bothered to head down to the desk. Some people just figured they had to take what came their way without even asking. And then they'd anonymously give us a horrible review for problems we didn't know we had.

"I only saw a couple walking out. They looked interested in what was going on across the way but didn't say anything," the officer said.

"Good. Good." I wanted to ask more, like whether or not he'd noticed anyone going back to the room beyond the suite but couldn't quite figure out how to ask. I mean, where did concern end and nosiness begin?

Olive probably would have asked and given him her opinion on all things legal and then left. I didn't quite have her gutsiness.

"Is there anything else?" the officer asked as I stood there debating.

"Not really," I replied. "I wanted to be sure that no one had any issues. I have someone in the room at the end of the hallway, as well." There that was general enough. Perhaps he'd share.

"We're keeping an eye out for her ma'am. She was the one who noticed the smell."

I nodded.

"It's odd, though isn't it? That a body would smell that strongly so quickly?"

The officer shrugged. He wasn't going to give me

anything. Perhaps Lyle would know more. He'd seemed willing to chat with me about what was happening.

I decided I'd heard down to my apartment and make some dinner. Something simple, which was all I ever did. I am not a fancy cook nor do I enjoy it much. I suppose that was one thing that made living on the premises bearable. I could easily grab a sandwich, burger, salad or any number of things, all on my walk downstairs.

I headed back down the hallway, my head filled with what I might ask Lyle when I called him, only to practically run into Detective Granger coming out of the elevator.

Chapter Fifteen

I'd barely gotten to the front of the elevators when the silvery doors slid open and Detective Granger stepped out. I didn't pause, intending to step past her as if this was a normal walk for me.

"What brings you up here?" she demanded.

"I wanted to be certain that your officers hadn't heard complaints from the people in the rooms across the way. Sometimes people will say something to those near them not realizing they don't work for the hotel. I'd hate to get a negative review over something preventable."

"You could have called up," Granger said.

"And interrupted them? I didn't even knock. I just talked to your officer."

Granger's eyes narrowed as if she were assessing whether this meant I was the killer.

"Stay out of this," she said before turning to leave. I got the faintest traces of cigarette smoke and mint as she turned. I hoped if she'd been smoking, she had taken it outside.

We'd talked just long enough for the elevator to have

made its way back down to the lobby so I had to wait while one of them ascended. I tried listening to what was being said around the corner, but short of poking my head out of the little alcove, I couldn't hear a thing. I sighed. Just my luck.

I didn't run into anyone on the way back down to my apartment. There, I tossed a couple of chicken thighs into the microwave with a nice sauce I'd found in the grocery store. Quick and easy. After I fed the cats, I put together a little salad. The two things were a nice simple dinner.

While I wanted to immediately call Lyle and find out what he might know about the investigation, I didn't want to be crunching on salad or chewing on the chicken while I talked so I ate first. The cats, although they'd just been fed, leapt up to sit next to me, their long Siamese noses sniffing hopefully in my direction.

Latte made a loud yowl when I finished the first piece, as if to remind me they were there and they were hungry. I mean, as if I could have missed them. Sometimes I think my cats think I'm an idiot.

After finishing my dinner, which I decided not to share given that the cats had been rather rude about demanding some, I cleaned up and then settled in to call Lyle.

Before I could do so, my cell phone rang.

"What is it?" I asked.

"Detective Granger wants to enter Catalina Thomas' room," Addy said.

"Why?" I mean, I could guess, but I couldn't imagine there was a reason for it.

"She said they called a cell phone number for Ms. Thomas and it rang in that room. They're concerned."

I sighed. There was the perfectly obvious reason that someone could have left their phone behind. On the other hand, the person next door to her had been murdered. Ms.

Thomas could have seen or heard something. Or she could have been that ex-wife and whoever killed Floyd didn't like her either. Hard to say.

"Tell her I'll be up with a master key. If we're going to get sued, it ought to be me in charge," I said.

After giving each cat a few ear rubs and a stroking the fur along their backs, I turned around and left the apartment. This wasn't an errand I wanted to do so I walked slowly. I could have Addy call our legal representative about whether or not we ought to allow the detective in, but at the same time, if Ms. Thomas had fallen, the delay could cost her her life.

The elevator stopped at the lobby and the detective waited at the elevator doors. She pushed past me and had the button pressed to close the doors before I'd managed to take a single step outside. I'd planned to have Addy call our attorneys to let them know my plans.

"I'll go in first. That way if the guest is in the room and unharmed, I have not let someone else trespass," I said. "She might be annoyed that a manager went in but given that her cell phone rang and wasn't answered, I can say we had some concerns."

Detective Granger gave me a thin smile. "Don't touch anything you don't have to in there," she said. "Did they get to you for the prints and DNA?"

I shook my head.

"Tomorrow then." She seemed largely unconcerned. Perhaps my dull lifestyle had been impressed upon her.

"I asked about this Olive woman you mentioned. Most people seem to think she's dead," Granger said.

The elevator doors opened to the top floor. The same recording was playing. I needed to see to it that the shuffle worked a bit better. I didn't want people coming upstairs and hearing the same thing every single time.

Perhaps Brandon could do something. He was my computer wiz.

"The manager before me was named Olive, yes," I said. I didn't add that she was also the person Granger had seen in my office.

I headed out the doors, walking quickly and purposefully around the corner. If Granger wanted to chat, she'd have to hurry to catch up. I am not tall, but compared to her, my legs had a lot more reach.

Normally, I wouldn't be that petty, but I did not want to chat about Olive.

I got to the door and knocked.

No answer, which wasn't a surprise. We were watching for Catalina.

I used my pass key and entered the room. The narrow entry prevented anyone from seeing what was around the corner. Something felt wrong, though. I stepped in, noting the bags on the luggage stand to one side. There was an odd smell amongst the usual aroma of cleansers that would normally permeate a room. Something slightly metallic.

Another step and I peeked around the corner.

Catalina lay on the bed.

I gasped.

I motioned to Detective Granger and then backed out of the room. My stomach was doing flips in a way it hadn't when I'd found Floyd. I think I'd been more shocked by finding him. Today, having just had that experience and half-expecting to see something horrible, it was less of an immediate shock and my stomach had decided it didn't like this particular situation.

Fortunately, getting out of the room and a few deep breaths settled my stomach enough that I wasn't going to make a fool of myself and potentially mess up a crime scene. I hadn't had time to notice much, but I had a feeling that Catalina was dead. There'd been blood and I hadn't heard the sound of any breathing.

I tried to remember if I could normally hear another person breathing, but I didn't often have the opportunity to come across someone napping. I leaned back against a wall, past the officer that Granger had ordered to seal off the room.

She was talking into a phone or radio or something and asked for the coroner again. Apparently, I'd been right. My brain had just shut out the image of that poor woman lying there.

Perhaps Catalina had reported Floyd's death too quickly. Or maybe she'd seen something she shouldn't have and only realized the significance of it after Floyd was dead. At any rate, whether she was or was not using a false name for Kate Thompson, she clearly wasn't the murderer.

Chapter Sixteen

The detective let me leave the floor, though she asked me stay in the hotel. I gave her my cell phone number so they could reach me if they had questions. I needed to get away. This morning, finding Floyd was one thing. Finding a second person did me in.

While part of me thought I should head down to my apartment to spend some time with my cats and get feline comfort, I ended up in the lobby bar. I had planned on going to the quieter mezzanine bar but the piano player had picked up quite a few fans and there wasn't a lot of space. While the music downstairs was louder than I wanted, the pop music a jarring counterpoint to the seriousness of the deaths upstairs, it was far less crowded.

I got a table towards the back, my preferred spot and immediately ordered one of their sangrias. I was thankful I'd managed to eat dinner earlier. I wouldn't be eating much afterwards at all. I drew in a few breaths trying to calm myself.

Teri came out and settled down with me, leaving Ryan to clean up the bar.

"You aren't my normal cliental," Teri said looking at me. She had a lemonade for herself.

"It's finding Floyd this morning. Now that poor woman who smelled something is dead as well," I said.

Teri raised an eyebrow.

"I had to let the police into her room. I went in first like a good manager and saw…"

It seemed both people had been murdered with a knife which led me to think it was the same person, though I couldn't be certain. I hadn't seen a knife in Catalina's room. I couldn't remember if I'd seen one in Floyd's and just assumed the blood was because he'd been cut. Still, the idea of two killers in the hotel seemed a bit much. It had to be the same person. She must have known something she shouldn't have or gotten in the way somehow.

"Sound horrible," Teri said. "I can't say that many of the employees are upset about Floyd, though. Those that didn't know him, don't feel like it affects them. The ones that did know him, well, they aren't upset for other reasons."

I nodded. That I could totally understand.

"Ryan, of course, is practically crowing," Teri went on.

"Why?" I asked. I wanted to know what Teri knew about Ryan and Floyd not getting along.

"Floyd comes in here when he stays and I think sometimes he goes out of his way to annoy Ryan. I've heard it's because Ryan worked another property and got canned for theft."

"You haven't had problems with Ryan here, though?" I pressed.

Teri shook her head. "If he was behind the theft, then he's really reformed. His till has never once been off. I've never seen him so much as pour an extra shot for someone.

Considering I heard Floyd accuse him of doing that, I made sure to watch."

"Like Floyd had it out for him," I said.

Teri nodded.

"Exactly. To his credit, Ryan has always acted professionally when Floyd's around. If he gets too hot about something, he asks someone to cover and takes a break. If I know Floyd is going to be here, I give him a couple of days off no matter how I have to juggle the schedule. It works. Unfortunately, no one knew Floyd was coming the other night."

"Not even me," I said. "And he wasn't pleased about not getting the Royal Suite."

Teri grinned. "This time, Ryan kind of lost it with him. Floyd was accusing him of drinking the alcohol instead of putting it in his drink. Ryan snapped at him and left without even asking if someone could cover. He didn't come back until it was practically closing."

"Did you say that to the police?" I asked.

"I wasn't going to, but that detective was asking some pretty specific questions. I hope she doesn't decide to set her sights on him. It's not as if he could have killed Floyd and just come back to work. He was in the same clothing he was wearing before he left. He stank like a chimney, though, so I think he was out smoking a pack or two to try and cool off."

I nodded. "Did you say that?"

"Absolutely," Teri said. "I'd be horrified to find out I'd hired a murderer so I can't believe Ryan would do something like that."

"I find it hard to believe that any one of our people would have done such a thing," I said. "Which leaves a guest, but if Floyd didn't tell us he was coming, who would he have told?"

"Unless there was a stalker," Teri said. "Maybe someone was following him around?"

"Maybe. But they'd have had to know how to hack into our system and shut down the camera in the hallway outside Floyd's room. It would be easier for an employee to do that."

"Like Ryan." Teri finished.

"Or someone in security." That person would have the easiest time. Which led me to think about Jake. I didn't want him to be the murderer, but he would have the easiest time hacking the computers. I couldn't see him sitting and having wine with Floyd. Unless he'd interrupted Floyd with Catalina. Maybe she was Kate and they'd hooked again for old times and Jake happened upon them. Perhaps she confronted him.

Teri watched me as those thoughts flitted through my mind. "I don't envy you wondering if someone here killed Floyd. Or his neighbor."

I made the appropriate noises though I said nothing. Teri was right on about my concerns.

"I wonder why someone would have murdered the woman next door. If she knew something, wouldn't she have said something right away?" Teri continued that line of thought.

"Maybe she didn't know she knew it?" I suggested. "Or maybe she only realized what she knew after finding out Floyd was dead. She left after telling us about the smell. I'm not sure when she came back, but by the time the police started looking for her, she had to be in her room."

"And whoever entered her room had to have killed her by that time or the police would have noticed someone leaving the room," Teri said.

"Maybe? It's not the only room down at that end. The people across the hallway are there because the hall itself isn't a crime scene or if it is, the police decided it wasn't worth the hassle of searching it because we had so many people there."

"It's possible if a guest saw something, they don't know what it was they saw. It's not like we advertised the crime, though it's probably obvious. Even so, a lot of people don't want to get involved," Teri said.

I sipped my sangria. The red wine was a little bit too overwhelming for the fruit flavors that evening. Or for what I was hoping for. I wasn't going to say that to Teri though.

We chatted about a few other things.

"Keep me posted about Ryan. I haven't noticed anything off on our larger numbers but it makes me wonder what Floyd really had against him," I said.

"Maybe he wanted Ryan to steal something and Ryan refused," Teri said. "He tried to get one our waitresses to bring him a full bottle of bourbon and pretend like he just got a single drink."

I raised an eyebrow.

"Yeah, I know. Makes you wonder, right?"

"It does indeed," I said. It wasn't impossible that Floyd was stealing from other people, which brought me back to Teri's suggestion of a stalker. Or, I thought, heart sinking again, Ari.

Talk about another person I didn't want to be the murderer. But it was certainly possible. Anything was. While Ryan might not have looked like he'd just killed someone, he had been gone while the murder was happening. He'd have access to hotel computers. If he was at all good with them, then he could have blanked out the camera.

Of course, a stabbing was bloody and Teri would have noticed if he'd changed his clothing. If he wore an older outfit just to kill Floyd, that would work, but that suggested premeditation.

I hated this. I wanted this to be someone I didn't know at all. And I wanted to know that fact right away. I didn't want to go on suspecting my workers.

Chapter Seventeen

The cats were not pleased with the way the evening was going. It had been decidedly unpredictable. I tried apologizing to them. I even pulled the crocheted afghan over my legs to entice them to cuddle with me. Latte gave me a long look from his place on the back of the sofa and yawned widely. I got a good whiff of cat breath before he left the room to saunter into the bedroom.

Chai hadn't even bothered to do that. He'd seen me come in and left the sofa to wander into the bedroom and up onto the bed. It was getting late. I turned on the television, hoping for something mindless to take my thoughts away from everything. I was in quite a spin as far as wondering who might have murdered Floyd and Catalina.

My cell phone rang. Lyle.

"What's up?" I asked. It was late for him to be calling.

"I found out a little about that car accident you asked me to look into," Lyle said. "I'd have waited until tomorrow but I have no idea how early Olive decides to pop in and bother you."

"Not usually very early but it will take my mind off of our last murder," I said.

"Al Granger isn't still giving you a hard time, is she?" Lyle asked, surprising me with the fact that he knew the detective well enough to use what was clearly a nickname.

"No but I found a guest dead in her room. She was the one who reported the smell that led us to Floyd's body." I swallowed after I spoke, hating to think of what I had seen.

"Really?" Floyd perked up. "Interesting. Do you think she knew something?"

"I'd hope so. Otherwise, we just have a murderer wandering around that floor killing people randomly." Which was something I hadn't thought of before. Perhaps I ought to make sure the people across the hallway were moved. And maybe everyone on that floor. I could just shut the entire hotel down for a week or so, but that would be horrible both for guests and for the publicity. *Hotel has serial killer* was not a headline I wanted to see connected to the Neary-Ten.

"Yeah. I guess the other options aren't very good, are they?"

I picked up my TV remote and turned the thing off. The paused image had been a close up of a man's face and it was starting to annoy me. His eyes appeared to be looking right at me as I talked to Lyle and I kept imaging that someone was listening in.

"I would hope there's not a serial killer here," I said.

Lyle chuckled slightly. "It's unlikely. That's not really how serial killers work, except maybe in bad fiction."

He knew I loved my mysteries and crime stories, so it annoyed me that he called them all bad fiction. Or maybe just those that dealt with serial killers. There'd been a lot of those lately, as if it was the only sort of killer bad enough for their various detectives.

"But what did you learn about Corbin?" I asked.

"The police thought maybe someone had run him off the road. However, a few days later someone came in and said that they'd killed a deer that looked as if it had been injured. Tracking backwards, the deer was probably hit on the road where Corbin was. The theory became that he swerved to avoid hitting the deer, didn't quite make it, and ended up hitting a tree and dying."

"That wasn't in the news," I said.

"I have contacts," Lyle told me. "It's the best I can do."

"I'll let Olive know," I said. "I think she was worried she'd murdered him. Corbin recognized her, you know."

"Was it weird for him to see her as a ghost?" Lyle asked.

"I think he was just surprised to see her. Maybe he didn't even register that she was a ghost. It's not like he's around all the time like most of our other spirits."

"True. It is weird that he remembered her. Or maybe not. Maybe she just made an impression on him."

"From what I've heard, he didn't seem all that well-liked. A guest found some articles from his former employer. They must have just scanned things in or something," I said.

"From what I gathered looking at the file downtown, no one had much good to say about him. He was difficult with everyone. His credit card was declined at the bar, though it went through at the main desk. He argued and almost got into a fight with the bartender at the time. The police were even called, though that was by the night manager and not Olive," Lyle said.

"But that wouldn't have endeared him to her," I said. "I bet she gave him a piece of her mind when he came down the elevator or when he checked out."

"Olive?" Lyle asked.

"I heard she'd had something of a drinking problem around that time, so her tongue was probably looser than it is now."

Lyle chuckled a bit. "I didn't know her then. I was new here and only here that time for a couple of years. I had to wander a bit before I decided that this was where I wanted to settle. There's enough civilization for me but also enough park to keep an eye on."

We talked a little more. I appreciated that his news seemed to exonerate Olive and I couldn't wait to tell her. I hoped she popped in soon so I could.

I was more relaxed after talking with Lyle and by the time I hung up, I was ready to actually watch a bit of television and settle in for the night.

I just hoped that I'd be able to sleep without having nightmares about finding dead bodies in hotel rooms.

Chapter Eighteen

The next morning, I was back at work after having slept surprisingly well. I did have one nightmare about finding another body, but it wasn't nearly as bad as it could have been. I could hardly remember the details when I woke, so I counted that as a win.

Suzanne was typing on her computer when I reached the main desk. I held up my cup of coffee in acknowledgement. She paused in typing to raise her own glass. Before I could say anything, she turned back to the computer. Something had probably just come in and she wanted to be sure it was noted before she got distracted.

I sipped my coffee, which tasted delightfully bitter, and set the mug down on my desk. I settled into my chair to check emails. While I'd checked before bed from my apartment, emails could come in at any time and who knew what was important. I always tried to read them and sort them so I knew what I had to do later.

While the day was promising to be bright and sunny and warmer than usual, again, my office was precisely as bright as always, though after the sunny lobby, it felt dark even with the light wood. We'd considered putting in a little window that looked out over the lobby for me but the cost was prohibitive. I wrinkled my nose at the stink of smoke. The office was not where I wanted to be that morning.

Fortunately, Suzanne poked her head inside.

"Addy left a message that the couples in the rooms on the top floor were asked to be moved downstairs by the police."

"All of the top floor or just Floyd's end?" I clarified. I'd hate it if our honeymoon couple was moved.

"Just those two up across from Floyd," Suzanne said. "I was double checking that when you came down."

"Any complaints?" I asked.

"Addy gave them both mini suites so they were fine."

"Good." I would have done the same. I was glad Addy had thought of it. "Anything else?" My fingers caressed the coffee mug as I considered whether I wanted another sip or if I would wait.

Suzanne shook her head. "I did get questioned by Detective Granger last night. She came down and found me in the conference room with Olive. I mean, Olive had just disappeared when we heard someone out there, but I got questioned."

"Anything I should know?" I hoped that Suzanne hadn't been asked about me. I would hate to think that the detective had focused on me as a suspect.

"She asked what I knew about Floyd. I told her about him arguing with someone on the phone earlier that evening. She seemed really interested. She also wanted to know who Olive was."

"What did you say?"

Suzanne sighed before speaking.

"I said that she's someone who used to work here. She

and I were working on a book so sometimes she's still around."

"I told her that Olive used to work here, too. And that she always seems to be around, but doubted that she saw anything as she'd have told me about it," I said. At least we'd gotten that part of our stories straight.

"She also asked me if Floyd had been mean to anyone in particular," Suzanne confessed. "I had to say he'd been quite rude to you when he checked in."

"As you should have. I mean, she needs to have all the facts. Anyone could have taken offense to what he said. I didn't murder him, obviously, but if you had left that out, it might have looked bad if someone else had mentioned it to her"

"Then she asked me if I knew if Ari was staying at the hotel." Suzanne looked puzzled as she said that.

"And?"

She shook her head. "I mean, I told her I could look in the computer but I hadn't seen her."

"Neither have I," I said. "I know that the detective said her cell phone was pinged in the area, but if she registered, she'd have done so in the evening. I'm not sure Addy knows what she looks like."

"I don't either," Suzanne said. "But it seemed a bit odd."

I had to agree. "Did she ask anything about Catalina Thomas?"

"Only if I remembered checking her in. I said I had done so the day before Floyd arrived and that she seemed really nice."

"Anything else?"

Suzanne shook her head. "Not anything specific. She asked me a lot of questions about what I thought of Catalina and stuff, but there wasn't anything that stood out to me. I mean, she wasn't ever rude or anything, just nice. It's not like we were friends. I just chatted a little with her while checking her in."

"True," I said. I wondered what Granger was after. I was surprised that she hadn't asked about the name and identity. Maybe she knew something about Catalina that I didn't. Like maybe Catalina was a fake name and her real name was Kate Thompson. Or not. Of course, if it was a fake name, Granger was in a far better position to know than my desk worker.

"You know, Ari said Floyd used to be married to someone named Kate Thompson. I wonder if Catalina could be a pseudonym for Kate."

"You mean like using the Spanish Catalina for Kate and a similar last name so it's easy to remember?" Suzanne said.

"Exactly."

"I could see it if it were one of Olive's books, but why would someone do that in real life? It's not like Floyd's not going to recognize her if he saw her. Well, unless she was also in disguise but she didn't look like she was. She looked normal."

My idea deflated. "I was just trying to fit the names into a box. They seemed awfully similar."

I heard the sound of the elevator doors opening and looked around. Jean was coming out. Her hair looked perfect. She wore sweats and a t-shirt and waved at us as she passed.

"An early morning swim before my massage!" she sang, as if we needed to know where she was going.

"Has she seen the ghost again, do you think?" Suzanne asked.

I had no idea, but I doubted it. I told Suzanne what we had learned about him. After that, I'd need to go update the website so people could learn a bit more about our ghost. After Jean left, I'd take a picture of the suite. It would allow us to show off our décor without looking like I was just advertising it if I referred back to the tale.

After we chatted about Corbin and the best way to tell the tale online—working with Olive had really honed Suzanne's editorial skills. I'd need to start sending her my articles before I posted them—I turned to go back to the office.

The front door opened and Detective Granger marched in with Detective Penn. Both of them headed directly for the front desk. I felt a slight headache coming on and I hoped that whatever they'd learned it wasn't something horrible.

Chapter Nineteen

My fingers stroked the warmth of my coffee mug as I breathed in the smell. You'd think that the caffeine in it would make me more anxious but I found the smell calming. Suzanne had also seen the detectives and I noticed she stood up straighter and pulled down her blue tunic top that she wore over her black jeans. We were fairly casual at the Neary-Ten. No need for formal uniforms.

While we had soft guitar music playing this morning, I still heard the click of heels on the hard floors as the two detectives crossed the room. I imagined a camera panning on them, their faces hard, watching us. Even Granger's feet, topped by her tiny little body, seemed to hit the floor with enough force that it should move, though it didn't. Larger humans than she had attempted to stomp across it.

"How can we help you today?" I asked them.

"Ariana Bowman," Granger snapped. "Where is she?"

"I haven't seen her," I said, my eyebrows furrowed.

"But you know she's here, right?" Penn asked a bit more kindly.

I shook my head. Suzanne did the same, looking as shocked as I felt.

"We pinged her phone again. And she's here. Either that or she's roaming the forest," Granger said.

"She's not here," I said. "It's possible she's visiting a guest but we wouldn't necessarily know that. We don't require everyone to sign in and out when they come in."

The look on Detective Granger's face suggested that she thought perhaps we should. Not that that would go over well. We were a hotel, not a prison.

I drew myself up and looked her in the eye. I hadn't heard from Ari since yesterday. I'd have thought she'd be upset about her brother. Why she'd be here and not say a word to any of us, I didn't know. I hated the way my stomach knotted in fear that perhaps she was the murderer.

"Search the place," Granger said. "And get the security camera footage."

I started to tell them they needed a warrant to take it away.

"Warrant." Granger held up a piece of paper.

It was late enough that Jake would be in, at least I hoped so. He'd read it and make sure it was fine. Still, I followed the detectives towards the elevator and joined them inside.

"Anything you want to share with us?" Granger demanded.

"Nothing that seems relevant," I said. "I just need to make sure your warrant is what you say it is and that we aren't offering anything we aren't supposed to."

Granger huffed.

Penn didn't say a word.

"You need to let us know what's going on whether you think it's relevant or not," Granger said. "Like the fact that you have employees who were basically being blackmailed by Floyd Bowman."

"What?" I asked, turning to her.

"Ryan Phillips your bartender," Granger said. "Bowman had worked with him one other time and Floyd had gotten him fired. Floyd kept threatening to have you look into what he was doing at the bar and get him fired again if he didn't serve him the way Floyd wanted."

"Teri, the head bartender, told me that story last night," I said. "I didn't know about it before. Whatever Floyd did to Ryan, nothing was flagged on our background checks when we hired Ryan as a bartender."

Penn made a note but didn't look at me. Granger stared at me as if trying to decide if I were hiding something, though why I would, I had no idea. It's not like I was close to Ryan's age and we were having a torrid affair.

"He'd have access to the security system, though," Granger said.

"Sort of. I think Jake said that if you knew what you were doing you could access the system from inside the hotel and take out the camera," I said.

"But it would be harder from outside," Penn added.

"I have no idea if Ryan has the computer skills."

"He has about a year of IT training under his belt. Made him dress up. Didn't much like it." Granger said all that without her usual attitude. Just the facts, ma'am.

"Teri does the hiring for the lobby bar," I said. "While I see the reports, I am not that hands on. I do get detailed reports that would show me if there were discrepancies or changes in what we're ordering or the money we're bringing in. Nothing changed after Ryan was hired. Both Teri and I would have noticed."

Penn made a few more notes.

The elevator doors slid open with a quiet hush. We

stepped out into the sub-basement. While it wasn't institutional it was far less nice than the main areas where guests might go, though definitely better than the concrete stairs that led down, which always made me feel as if I were in some sort of industrial wasteland. We had to walk down the hall and around the corner to the security offices, passing the employee elevator and the hated back stairs.

Brandon was at the front desk. He raised an eyebrow to see the two detectives.

"They have a warrant to see the footage from the security camera on the top floor hallway," I said.

"Actually, all the cameras," Granger said. "We have some extra hands who will be going through it."

"Then all the footage," I said.

Granger handed me the warrant and I skimmed through it. I was not an attorney but I wanted to be sure it said all the cameras, which it did. And I wanted to be sure it wasn't just a blank piece of paper that Granger was telling me was a warrant. It was the sort of thing I wouldn't put past her. But it looked as if everything was in order, or close enough that no one was going to have a fit if we gave out our video footage, except maybe our attorneys, but that's what they were paid to do.

Brandon started typing on the screen. I heard a ping down the hallway above the soft rock they were playing in the office. Granger looked around, taking in the plain floors and the small reception area with its undecorated walls and the hallway that would wind its way down through what everyone affectionately called the maze.

A few minutes later, Jake walked out. He moved a bit more slowly than usual. He held a thumb drive in his hand.

"Here's the footage from the top floor that Detective Penn and I watched," he said. "It will take some time to download all the video, but I should have it in a couple of hours if you want to come back?"

Granger looked like she was about to argue but Penn nodded at Jake. "We can start with this, thanks."

Jake nodded. I watched the two detectives leave. I figured they knew the way out. If they had more stuff to do, then they'd stick around. I had no desire to hang out with Detective Granger any longer than I had to. Perhaps that was why she was so difficult. She put off people she didn't want to have to deal with.

"I ought to tell you something," Jake said. He gestured down the hallway towards his office. I followed him down the hall, which was narrower than most halls in the hotel. His shoulders practically brushed the gray cubical walls that lined the way.

Olive picked that moment to pop in, lowering the temperature in an already cool area markedly. I shivered.

"You'll never guess what I learned!" she clapped her hands together.

"What?" I asked.

"I got in the elevator with those two detectives. Did you know that Catalina Thomas was not who she said she was?" Olive asked, staring at me.

"I suspected it was a fake name for Kate Thompson, Floyd's ex-wife," I said.

"Oh it was, sort of. Actually, the woman killed was Kate's friend Wendy Wickstrom. Apparently, Kate and she enjoyed having a girl's spa holiday together. They checked in the day before Floyd. They were in the lobby bar when Floyd arrived. Kate immediately packed her bags and left. She didn't cancel the room so that Wendy could enjoy the rest of the time. Floyd didn't know her and would have no reason to ruin her holiday." Olive looked pleased with herself.

"That's weird," Jake said. He started to say something else but Olive cut him off.

"It's perfect for my next novel. I'm already planning it out." She sounded so excited about fact that Catalina wasn't who we thought she was. I tried to remember if Suzanne had asked for a name or if she'd just used the computer and saw who it was. Or maybe Wendy had used Catalina's name, figuring if Floyd figured out who it was, then she'd get better treatment.

"Why use a fake name?" Jake finally asked.

"I heard from the detectives, after they left the elevator of course," Olive said smugly, "but I followed a little behind them. Catalina is Kate's real name. And she uses Thomas because it's so similar to Thompson. Most people don't look that closely at ID and she just explains the first name and they overlook the slightly different last name. She nearly always uses her real name, however, when she stays somewhere Floyd might have access to records—as if —she uses that name."

I raised an eyebrow. I'd have to talk to whoever checked her in.

"But isn't it a great idea?" Olive pressed. "Is it too much of a twist?"

"Olive," I said gently. "This isn't a book. Two people are dead."

"So am I," Olive replied pointedly, daring me to say something to that.

"She's got you there," Jake chuckled, turning back to his computer to get going on copying more video for the police.

"You were going to tell me something?" I asked Jake.

He shook his head and just said, "It's not important right now."

I waved at him and walked out into the hallway maze. Olive followed along, keeping me cool.

"I really don't know why they didn't let you build out real offices and maybe a normal hall when you had work done down here," Olive said. She was referring to some work that had been done in the sub-basement about a decade ago. We'd expanded the offices into what had once been a storage section. It meant we had to be more cautious with keeping extra tables and chairs but ultimately with sorting through stuff and not keeping so many extras on hand, we worked it out.

"They were used to their offices," I said quietly, thinking.

Wendy couldn't have been the intended victim on her own. She had to have been killed because the murderer thought she knew something. If she did, she didn't know it, or else she'd been killed before she could share it with anyone.

"I forgot to ask Jake if he saw anyone going into Catalina's—I mean Wendy's—room," I said.

"If he had, don't you think he'd have said something immediately?"

Brandon was still at the desk. I paused.

"Do you know if the police saw anyone going into Catalina's room before she was killed?" I asked.

"That camera fritzed out again. Someone messed with it big time. It glitched again just a few hours ago, which was after everyone was moved out of that area," he said. "Whoever was messing around must have left some sort of artifact in the code. I was going to look for it, but Jake wanted the police to take care of that first."

I smiled and nodded, not willing to say anything to Brandon. But Jake had had words with Floyd. Now he didn't want

Brandon looking at video footage. Of course, he was right about Detective Penn saying the police needed to check first, but I suspected that Brandon would have been rather discrete.

"I wonder if there was something in the room," Olive said. "Or maybe the person thought there was something in the room that they needed."

"Or they were checking for something they worried they dropped?" I asked. "But I can't imagine what it could be. The police forensics unit would have taken anything suspicious."

"Maybe it wasn't something suspicious, exactly," Olive said. "We have plenty of shampoo and soaps. Perhaps the person used the soap and was worried their DNA would be left behind."

"Or they showered off and were worried about the shampoo and hoped it was still there?" I asked.

"Or they dropped an earring. That's what always happens in your crime shows." Olive often dropped in to watch television with me. At least she did before she began editing her novel with Suzanne.

We walked up the back stairs, or rather I walked and Olive glided. I was thankful to get to a warmer part of the hotel so that the chill coming from Olive wasn't quite so intense.

"If it was an earring, they were probably out of luck. The police would have found it," I said.

"Or maybe they planted an earring to make it look like someone else did it. You for example," Olive pointed out.

That would make more sense. They'd want to be sure the police found whatever it was they dropped.

"If it was an earring, then they could be trying to frame Ari."

"Why on earth would they want to do that?"

"Maybe they have something against the Bowman's.

Or maybe having met Floyd, they don't believe the rest of the family would be any better?" I suggested.

"I'm not sure how the whole family could be that bad," Olive said. She glanced back at the elevator perhaps wondering why I didn't take it up to the next floor.

"Perhaps I could go in and find something. I'll go have a look around. If there's no one in the room, I can try and listen and see if there's something going on nearby."

Olive popped out as I started up the main stairs to the lobby. I shook my head thinking about her sudden interest in crime. She'd been so excited about telling me about Wendy that I'd forgotten to tell her about Corbin's crash.

Chapter Twenty

Upstairs, I noted Mark was at the desk but Suzanne wasn't around. She was probably on break. I breathed in the smells of early morning baking from the lobby bar. It was light and fresh and only faintly pizza-ish, if that was such a word. Underlying that was the usual fresh, clean scent from our janitorial workers.

Sun radiated through the big front windows. The HVAC was blowing down on me from the high ceiling, though I could barely feel it. The room would be warm that day. We had more vents in the floor along the wall, fortunately, and one behind the desk. Those were put in some time after the major remodel when it was determined that the air didn't quite circulate enough in the lobby.

I tapped my foot to a jaunty guitar tune. It was clearly the same playlist that Suzanne had selected this morning, only this tune was a bit more upbeat. It was a nice change from what we'd been listening to. I ought to make a note to myself to change it up again tomorrow. I spent so much time absorbed in my work in my office, where I often had my own music on a low volume that I'd forget about the main lobby. Not that people came to the hotel to listen to music, but all the same, I wanted everyone to have a good experience.

"Anything new?" I asked Mark.

"No new dead people if that's what you're asking," he said. "A detective asked about who could have been messing with the cameras again and if there was any way for us to monitor that. I told them they'd need to talk to Jake. That got some strange looks."

I raised an eyebrow. I wondered if someone else had overheard Jake and Floyd talking. Perhaps someone had already mentioned his altercation to the police. If so, no one had questioned me. Even if someone had overheard Jake and Floyd, perhaps they hadn't noticed me in the hallway outside.

"Yeah, I thought that was odd, too. I mean, if they didn't think Jake could do it, then I'd have thought they'd just go to you."

"I took the detectives down earlier with a warrant for the videos. Jake had the camera from the top floor ready for them. He's working on the rest."

Mark nodded. "It seems weird that they didn't ask him about the security cameras and figuring out who could have gotten to them while they were there."

"I know they asked him the first day. He said pretty much anyone."

"But Brandon is probably pissed off that he doesn't know where it came from," Mark pressed.

"Jake told him not to go investigating, to leave that to the police."

Mark frowned. I was glad I wasn't the only one who found that strange. At least I hadn't mentioned Jake's altercation with Floyd. I drew in a breath. I did not want to think about my head of security being a murderer, no matter how much Floyd might have deserved it.

"Did they say anything else?" I asked.

Mark shook his head.

"When they first interviewed you, what did you tell them about Olive?" I asked. It would be a good idea to get a sense of what the employees were saying about her. Should I ever have to explain her presence to the police again, I wanted us all to be consistent.

"Only that she used to be the manager here," he said. "I omitted that she was dead. I figured if they knew about her, they might have seen her and I didn't want them going off on a tangent looking for the woman impersonating her."

I smiled. An interesting idea.

My phone rang and I looked down at the number. Ari's name showed up.

"I need to take this," I told Mark and headed into the office.

Answering, I waited to hear what Ari had to say.

"I've been told the police are looking for me there," she said.

"They said they pinged your cell phone and it came up as being here," I said.

"Let me call you right back," Ari said before hanging up.

As I knew from experience, Ari calling me right back could mean in an hour. I was already seated at my desk, so I pulled up my work task list and the notes that I'd left for myself from the day before. I needed to remind myself of everything that I needed to juggle and what days I needed to do it. I couldn't exist without my task list.

Olive had poopoo-ed the idea of a task list. I had no idea how she did it but I had to admit, I'd been impressed with how efficient she was as a manager. She might not have been as creative as I like to think I am, but she'd been in the job for a very long time. No doubt she didn't feel she had to be creative to get things done.

Surprisingly, it was only fifteen minutes later that Ari called me back. I considered sending the call to voicemail as I wasn't familiar with the number. But between Ari and the police, I figured I really ought to answer.

"Okay, I think I can talk now. I shut off my phone," she said.

I considered asking her why she didn't want the police knowing where she was but decided that I ought to warm her up first.

"What's going on?" I asked.

"To be honest, I'm rather embarrassed. I'm involved with a man in the area, and well, I didn't want anyone to know. It's delicate." Ari sounded embarrassed even to mention that.

"I can't imagine why. It's not as if anyone is going to judge you. This isn't the 1950s." Ari might be slightly older than I was but she still deserved to have fun if she wanted to.

"Well, he's young," she said. "Younger than I am, I should say. By a lot. But we really connect, you know? And he's not really someone my family would consider suitable, either. He's not in business for himself."

Ari was embarrassed about her family finding out. I wondered if Floyd had followed her to the Neary-Ten. That could be a motivation for murder. My heart sank. I so did not want Ari to be the murderer. Of course, I thought that about pretty much everyone who had been on the short list of possible suspects.

"Did Floyd find out?" I asked.

"I think he suspected something. I have a feeling he

had something on my phone so that he could see where I was. I think that might be why he was at the hotel," Ari said.

"Did you know Kate was supposed to be here that weekend?" I asked.

"Kate? His ex?" Ari asked.

"She goes by Catalina. I didn't put it together until Olive overhead the police talking. She was coming with a friend. I guess the friend was the one who smelled something which is how we found Floyd." I winced as I spoke. First, I'd lied about not putting things together and then I'd been completely tactless about telling Ari how we found her brother.

"I had no idea," Ari said. "But Kate wasn't there?"

"She saw Floyd and left. I'm sure the police are checking to be sure she was gone when she said she'd be gone," I said.

"I'm sure." Ari sounded thoughtful.

"Also, Suzanne heard Floyd arguing with someone by phone. I have no idea who that was."

"If she told the police, they've probably already hunted down that number to see if the person was local or not," Ari said. "I ought to come clean and let them know where I was. I've contacted an attorney, though, just in case. I hope she'll be willing to help us keep this discrete."

"I hope so, too," I said. I really did. Of all the Bowmans, if Floyd was the most annoying, Ari was the nicest. The other sister was the one who had all these ideas that would cost a lot of money and not bring in much revenue. The other two brothers both thought they knew more than anyone about making money, though they frequently tended to side with the sister. It took a lot of effort to push them back into their places as owners rather than managers.

Annoyingly, the sister often hated my ideas, feeling they were, as she put it, too common. Floyd would then come up with his less common ideas, although the sister often hated his suggestions as well. Fortunately, she didn't often bother with the day-to-day management the way Floyd tried to.

We didn't talk much longer and I hung up, thoughtful. I jumped when the phone rang again. This time it was Lyle.

"What it is?" I asked. It didn't not appear I was going to get much done that day at all.

"I continued looking into Corbin Moore," Lyle said. "I may need to talk to your detectives about this."

"Why is that?" I asked.

"I'm giving you this head's up so I don't blindside you," Lyle said. "But one of the people interviewed after Moore's death was Floyd."

My mouth dropped and flapped around like a dying fish as I attempted to wrap my mind around that bit of information. I had no idea how long I sat there trying to process it while Lyle called my name from the other end.

I finally managed to speak as this new piece of information came to light. We needed to know more about our ghost in room 785.

Chapter Twenty-One

My office felt smaller than usual and darker, as Lyle reiterated what he knew. The cigarette smoke seemed stronger, as if every manager who had smoked their lungs into oblivion in the office were sitting there listening in on the conversation. Given that the Neary-Ten was haunted, perhaps they were. I mean, it's not like all ghosts were the same. Maybe these ghosts just didn't appear.

That idea made my heart palpitate, which was not what I needed so I attempted to push it away and listen to Lyle's voice telling me what he had found out.

"Floyd was there that weekend. And he left before the initial questioning. The police finally caught up with him at home, but only because Olive had mentioned he had returned there," Lyle said.

"And?" I had sudden visions of Floyd murdering Olive in a fit of pique, though I knew her death had been due to a heart attack. Floyd hadn't been anywhere around.

"Apparently several workers had heard Corbin and Floyd arguing. I guess Corbin was complaining about how dull the resort was. If he was going to go to a luxury spa and resort in the middle of nowhere, he wanted something nice. Floyd took issue with that and the two had words. A few of the people described the two men as nearly coming to blows," Lyle said.

"Why didn't you notice this before?" I asked.

"Because once the police found out about the deer, they filed this in the back, as if it wasn't important," Lyle said. "I just thought it was interesting that a guy killed in an accident would haunt his room."

Which was a very good question. Most ghosts haunted the places they died, or were murdered. Some had more freedom to move around but they still seemed to tethered to their place of death.

"Plus, he doesn't show up often," I said. "I wonder if the other sightings of him were at times when Floyd was around. I just figured he showed up because it was the anniversary of his death, but I didn't even look."

"Don't know about that," Lyle said. "Did you ever keep a calendar?"

"I'd just hear things after the fact. It was always a guest saying they saw him or wanted to see him, but no one ever told me exactly when," I said. "He was always our mysterious ghost."

Lyle made an humph sound as if ghosts shouldn't be mysterious. It wasn't as if we were studying them, though I had people come *to* study them. Sometimes our ghosts cooperated and sometimes they didn't. Olive had had great fun with a paranormal investigator who had all this equipment and she walked around with him asking him questions.

He'd been fascinated by the fact that the hotel seemed to be one big cold spot and wherever he went the equipment went wild, but he reported that he'd never seen a ghost. Olive had gotten a kick out of that.

To be fair, most people think of ghosts as not looking quite solid. That's how they portray them in the movies. Olive looks normal though the air gets cold around her and she has a tendency to glide. If you look closely at her feet, you'll see that they just seem to leak into the floor, the soles of her shoes not being terribly solid.

She can sit if she wants to, though she's posing more than anything. At those times, she can make her feet look more solid. She's said she needs to concentrate a bit more, though.

"I'll be calling Granger so they can check out this Corbin Moore and see if he has any relatives who happen to be staying at the hotel," Lyle said.

"You do that," I told him, though I was already itching to get my hands on my computer to do some sleuthing.

Hanging up, I bit my lip. I needed to do some work. Many things could be put off, but I hated to get too far behind and I'd spent way too much time this morning poking my nose into things that were better left to the police. I did, however, appreciate Lyle's heads-up. I had no idea how I was going to explain our ghost to Detective Granger if she asked about him.

The music from the lobby helped to keep me focused on some of my tasks. However, it wasn't long before I wanted to know more about Corbin Moore. I hadn't found much on him when I'd searched for him in a general search. However, my sister had done one of those geological family trees. I had a login so I could look at it and fill information as I wanted.

I went there and searched for his name. I found several families with a Corbin Moore as part of their tree. I found a tree with a correct date of death. While I was able to find out other deceased family members, the living members names were hidden. So much for that idea.

Sighing, I prepared to get back to work. As I was about to close out the tab, I realized that Corbin had had a younger sister who had died just a year and a half ago. Chances were there'd be information online about her. I made a note of her name.

Before I got the chance to search, Detective Granger appeared in my doorway.

"Can I help you?" I asked looking up.

Mark stood behind her, his tall, thin frame practically towering over the petite detective. He was making faces so I knew he hadn't just let her in, she'd found the door and walked through without asking.

"Corbin Moore? I hear he and Floyd had words before he died," she said. "You're the ghost expert and supposedly you had a sighting the other day."

"It's actually the first time we've seen him," I said. "I assumed that many of the reports of a ghost in room 785 had been people with overactive imaginations, but our current guest called down when he appeared. I was able to get a name from him before he faded out."

Granger's expression didn't change. I had no idea how much she believed and how much she was humoring me.

Finally, she spoke.

"You see the ghosts yourself. You don't just rely on other people's reports?" she asked.

"We do both here. I've posted information about the ghost in room 785, which turns out to be Corbin Moore. I also post information on other ghosts that I have seen, like Clara down in the basement. She frequently appears running down the hallway as if someone was chasing her. There's also Smithers, a ghost who appears in the restaurant." I considered whether I ought to mention Olive. I'd leave her out of that discussion.

Granger's eyes narrowed. I wondered if she was debating having me committed. Of course, so many others at the hotel had seen the ghosts. They'd back me up.

"I'd like to know how you pull off these ghosts," she said.

"We don't pull off anything," I replied. "We've had ghost hunters come here. Some get lucky and find a ghost or two. Others miss them altogether. There are plenty of reports about us and our hauntings online. We're on all the major social media with links to the various reports. The highlights of our hauntings are also linked on our website if you want to read more."

Granger looked skeptical. Not that I blamed her. Although, living in the town, she should have heard that the Neary-Ten was haunted.

"Do you really believe the ghost killed Floyd Bowman?" she asked.

I frowned. I hadn't even considered that. "No. Not at all. I mean, I'm not an expert, but none of the other ghosts here are really able to influence anything physical. I've never seen one knock something over or open a door, for instance."

Of course, the only one who might want to was Olive and she couldn't. That didn't mean none of the others could. Smithers in the restaurant might want to, but again, I'd never known him to try. Clara ran on her little track and that was it. Angus, of course, just stared in the window. If he could change things, he'd probably open the door and come in out of the storm but the poor spirit was doomed to repeat his death in a snowstorm staring in the windows from the outside.

"But you said you saw Corbin Moore's ghost and spoke to him. Was that the day Floyd was killed?"

"It was the day before," I said. "We had a lovely woman check in and she saw him. She was quite startled. I'd wanted to know more about him because people love hearing about our ghosts, so having a name was very helpful. I've been working on writing up a bit of information so people can read about him on the website, now."

"And you weren't afraid? What about your guest?" Granger asked. This seemed to perplex her. I couldn't imagine her being afraid of anything but I'm not sure why it surprised me that she appeared to think others should be.

"When you work in a haunted hotel, you stop being afraid of ghosts. Like I said, mostly they create a chill in the air and maybe talk to you. They can't really interact with anything in the world."

"You're a true believer," Granger mused.

"I've experienced them," I said.

She gave me a long look as if wondering whether I was a fool or perhaps who could have pulled off a haunting that fooled even the hotel's manager.

"We'll be looking into Mr. Moore's family. Perhaps there was more to his death than hitting a deer."

"Perhaps," I said.

"Your former manager, Olive isn't around, is she?" Granger asked. "Perhaps she remembers Moore."

"I don't know what she knows," I said. "And I haven't seen her this morning."

"You do know she's dead, right?" Granger asked. "But you act as if she's a living person, who hangs around the hotel all the time."

"Well, she does hang around all the time. You, yourself,

saw her in my office and asked who she was. It didn't seem right to lie about who was in there."

Granger's face reddened slightly before she turned and left the room, clearly not pleased with how the interview had gone. From my point of view, it had gone better than expected. I mean, at least she hadn't started laughing. On the other hand, she did look rather angry, which might have been worse.

Chapter Twenty-Two

Although I was unsettled after talking to Detective Granger, I did manage to get myself to do some work. The music got louder and the scent of bar food got stronger as more people ate lunch and the day wore on. My stomach growled, reminding me that although I was still a little behind on my work, I needed to eat.

I stood and went to check on the front desk. Mark was going over some reports in the staff area next to my office. It was a private space but I liked to have someone actually at the desk lest a guest need assistance. Suzanne was monitoring the reception area and doing some cleaning up. I appreciated that she was good at keeping herself busy with things that made the hotel look good.

"I'm going to head down to my apartment for lunch," I told her and headed out. I enjoyed eating at home. I had sandwich fixings, as always, and I could spend some time with my cats.

I walked over towards the main stairwell that led down to the basement. An elderly couple walked by, both wore nice trousers and button-down shirts. It was warm for the long-sleeves they had and the Neary-Ten was not usually so formal, but perhaps they always dressed that nicely.

She smiled at me and I smiled back.

"A lovely hotel," she said, pausing noting my attention.

"Thank you," I said. "I hope you're having a lovely stay."

"Mostly. Of course, it's warmer than I expected or remembered. We were married here when we were young. Thirty-four years ago last month." She looked proud. Her husband looked a little confused. I wondered if he had a level of dementia. I hoped that wouldn't happen to me. I would hate to become a burden on someone.

I had no children to take me in or to send me to a facility, so I would have to do it myself if something happened. Watching people as they fell prey to the disease, I wondered if I would notice. The gentleman didn't seem to. He rubbed at his face and looked down at his shoes.

"It is warm today. We've been having an unseasonable month. I hope that we don't suddenly have a cold July or something," I said, still smiling.

The old woman nodded. "I love the mountains. We're from down in Charlotte and it's so flat there. At one time we talked about retiring to the mountains but time passed and we never quite got around to it. Now, we have to have doctors nearby so the city is really the place to be."

I nodded. I could understand that. It wasn't a long drive to the clinic from here. We had a couple of clinics in town and a division of a hospital, but for a larger hospital it was either Boone or go all the way to Raleigh. I know for more major things many people just went to Raleigh.

The couple moved on and I was able to walk down the stairs. They'd have been in Corbin Moore's age range had he lived. I might not be young, but I was compared to them. I hadn't lived in the southeast at that era so wasn't sure what life was like there then. I'd been safe in the Pacific Northwest, in my home, with my sister and my parents.

I wondered who Corbin Moore might have traveled with. It wasn't as if the Neary-Ten was the sort of place that people went to alone. Perhaps more so now, with the spa, but usually, unless it was for business, in those days people would have traveled with family or a loved one.

When I got to my apartment, I fixed myself a quick sandwich and gobbled it down. I settled in with the cats and called Lyle.

I was in luck. He picked up.

"Just can't get enough of me?" he joked. We didn't usually talk on the phone multiple times a day.

"I was thinking about Corbin Moore," I said. "It seemed like he was alone in the car. Why was he up here then? I mean in that era, I thought most people traveled with their family."

I knew Moore had family, though if he were married, she was still alive because I hadn't seen a name on a family tree. There was a blank spot. Also, a couple of blank spots for children and even grandchildren. The whited-out areas meant someone existed but those names weren't public.

"Probably," Lyle said slowly. "The reports made it sound like he was leaving but maybe they were mistaken? Or maybe I misread."

I heard him moving some stuff around and then reading.

"It says here he was leaving the hotel." Lyle sounded perplexed and then read some more. He made a few hmm noises that I suspected he was only doing so I knew he hadn't hung up on me.

"Yeah. Okay. It looks like he got in an argument with

his wife and she called a cab to take her to Boone to catch a bus. It seems she had two children with her," Lyle said.

"Did they say what the argument was about?" I asked.

"Just notes about domestic dispute. They highlighted no violence," Lyle said. "Her name was Jean but they don't list the children's names."

I could look up a Jean Moore, although I'd probably never get the right one. The name was common and even knowing she'd lived in Charlotte wouldn't help that much. Charlotte was a huge city.

"I wonder why they didn't add the children's names," I said.

"Probably too young to be suspects?" Lyle said. "Although it seems like the police had originally thought the crash was suicide, so they probably wanted to protect the family. It wasn't that long ago, but suicide still had a stigma. I mean, it still has one for some people."

"Detective Granger questioned me about Corbin Moore's ghost," I said. "She wanted to talk to the guest in that room but I'm not sure I ought to give out a name. It's not like they can interview a ghost, particularly not one who only shows up once in a while."

"She needs to be thorough," Lyle said. "I expect talking to the guest in 785 isn't high on her list, though. While Corbin was linked to Floyd, it's not like he could have murdered him. And Floyd has stayed at the hotel before, so even if the ghost could actually murder someone, Moore had other chances."

"I think if any of our ghosts could touch something, it would be Olive," I said. "She has the most presence, wandering around the halls wherever she wants. I doubt someone like Corbin Moore who just shows up in a room on rare occasions would be able to do such a thing."

"I don't actually pretend to know anything about ghosts," Lyle said.

"The woman who stayed in the suite seemed to know a bit about them. She likes hauntings. Maybe she knows more," I said. "I'll make a point to look her up when she's out and about. I think I saw her heading over to the spa earlier, so I can't just ring her up or anything. But maybe she has ideas."

"Sounds like a plan," Lyle said. "Hopefully she'll be willing to chat."

"She's been very friendly," I said. "I have no doubt she'll talk to me."

Lyle and I talked a bit more about a few things. He rang off and I settled in with Chai and Latte. Latte was on the arm of the sofa, his back to me watching the birds outside the window. Chai was on the back of the sofa, his back feet pressed against my neck as he watched the same birds.

I fiddled around with my phone trying to search Jean Moore. Even putting in the year that Corbin died, I didn't get anything worthwhile. I got a lot of offers for places to help me track her down but that wasn't really my goal. I tried putting in her name and obituary and the location as Charlotte but even that got me more results than I wanted to slog through on my phone. On the larger computer upstairs, or even my laptop, I might have done.

Instead, it was going to have to wait.

The rest of my lunch was spent reading up on ghosts and what might make a ghost haunt a certain place. Sadly, the articles didn't enlighten me on anything I didn't already know. After petting the cats for a bit and talking to them about the sorts of things one talks to their cats about, such as how rude the birds were being by troubling them out there, I stood up to head back to the front desk.

Olive was waiting outside the door.

"Good afternoon," I said. "What were you up to?"

"Trying to learn something more about Wendy, but unfortunately, the detectives that are wandering around are moving too much for me to try and follow. They aren't interviewing people as they were. It seems like they're just wandering around," she said.

"I didn't get a chance to tell you the other day, but I learned something about Corbin Moore," I started. Then I told her quickly about his accident and the deer. I added in that Corbin and Floyd had had an argument, which some reports said that they nearly came to blows.

Olive's eyes widened. "You know, I do recall a time when security was called on Floyd. It was in the restaurant if I recall. But he and another man were arguing about something stupid. The person Floyd was arguing with had reserved the table Floyd wanted, and you know how he is, he just brushes by what anyone else wants. I guess this man wasn't standing for it and started arguing with him. Security had to be called to break it up."

"It wasn't anything personal?" I asked. "Just an argument about who got a particular table?"

I knew which table. It was sort of off to the side and had windows on two sides instead of just one. It was a bit more private. We often put families there because the kids would be less disruptive. However, other times, guests requested that table simply because it was cozy place to eat.

Olive shrugged.

"Detective Granger asked me about Corbin Moore because Lyle told her what he'd found in the old case, saying it was strange that the ghost had just shown up. Then I had to talk to her about our ghosts. I'm not sure she thinks I'm completely sane. But she does know you're a ghost now," I said.

"Well, no help for that. I can always say boo if she starts looking a bit too nervous." Olive smiled, clearly pleased with herself.

We were still in the hallway outside my apartment. I started walking slowly towards the main stairs. I preferred the stairs to the elevator as that made sure I always got enough exercise. I might not get the recommended amount of vitamin D from the sun, but I definitely moved enough.

"But how would Corbin have factored into Floyd's death?" Olive asked, frowning.

"Well, she did ask me if we thought the ghost had done it. Of course, I explained that ghosts couldn't usually interact with physical things so he probably couldn't murder Floyd, but perhaps there's someone in his family that's here."

"Did he have family?"

"Lyle found the old reports. He had a wife named Jean and two kids that weren't named. I'm sure it had something to do with them thinking the accident was a suicide until they learned about the deer. Then it was just an accident and there was no reason to name the children. They would have thought the kids didn't know anything."

"That's very poor judgement. I think children often know more than adults because no one notices that they're listening and watching. You get fresher eyes. One of my best witnesses in my cozy novel is a child." Olive did her look down her nose at me thing as she fingered her pearls.

"You have to admit that it's strange that Corbin haunts room 785. He didn't die there," I said.

"Nor was his fight with Floyd there, which would have been an emotional thing." Olive frowned, looking thoughtful.

"Floyd would have been able to find out what room he was in," she went on. "It was even more difficult to stand up to him back then when he was younger. If anything, he's mellowed with age, though I realize he was still horrible. I'm sure it's hard to imagine him being worse but I think he was. Today, he wouldn't have nearly come to blows. You said he was even willing to take the owner's suite when he wanted the royal suite."

"He could have found out Corbin's room number and they did come to blows. Maybe Corbin was injured and that's why he was driving so poorly?" Olive asked.

It wasn't impossible.

"It was morning, if I recall," I said. "Although, I think the wife and kids had already left. She took a cab to the bus station."

"She must have gone to the one in town, because it would have taken her half a day to get to the one in Boone. Of course, if she took a cab from here to Boone, the cabbie would have made a pretty penny." Something I hadn't considered.

"I wonder what happened between the two of them."

"I suppose that's not the sort of thing one can find out on the computer," Olive mused. "Too bad. It might shed some light on that haunting."

I nodded and continued on, thoughtful.

Chapter Twenty-Three

I continued back up the stairs to work while Olive remained down in the basement, probably popping in where no one would notice her. We didn't have anything special going on. Our next conference wasn't until next month when we had a group of people who called themselves cryptid hunters staying there. I hadn't heard of the conference before. It was being arranged by a paranormal museum a few hours away.

They had a bunch of requests that they thought were special but weren't actually very difficult for us to provide. I knew Olive was looking forward to hanging out with the hunters to find out what they meant by cryptids. I'd looked up the term online for her but she still wasn't quite sure what they meant.

Detective Penn was at the desk talking to Mark. Mark wasn't a short man, but he was slender and at this angle, Penn seemed to tower over him. Mark didn't look particularly happy. Suzanne was helping a woman at the far end of the desk, as if she were trying to distance herself from the detective.

I hurried over there, moving quickly, wishing the lobby bar wasn't playing Madonna quite so loudly so I could hear the conversation sooner. I glanced over at the bar and noticed a half a dozen people in shorts and t-shirts all with drinks and a large pizza. Two women were dancing next to their table. I wished if they were going to dance this early that they'd at least head over to the little dance floor area.

Not that anyone was going to say anything. The women were not out of control and flailing around. We kept an eye on dancers like that, but only stepped in if they were likely to hit someone or hurt themselves if they hit something on the walls.

"Can I help?" I asked coming up to Mark.

Penn glanced over. I smelled cigarette smoke from him. In fact, if I were a smoker, I'd have gotten my hit just standing there.

"I was asking about the videos that Jake was supposed to get us."

"I can call down and see what's going on," I said, ready to step around the desk and do so.

"I can't get a hold of him," Mark said. "Brandon said he stepped out for a minute. He took the thumb drive he was going to give the police with him."

Penn eyed me as if wondering what I thought. On the one hand, it didn't look good for Jake. I had heard him arguing with Floyd. On the other hand, I couldn't see him killing someone. Not really. If Floyd had been beaten up and maybe died accidentally, I might consider Jake but I couldn't see him using a knife on someone.

"Do you think someone knew what he had and wanted to keep him from sending it to you?" I asked. My stomach twisted in worry. In some ways, it would be easier to say Jake was the murderer.

"I don't know," Penn said. "Do you? Or is it possible,

he's the murderer and realized he forgot to hide something from the camera?"

Penn leaned against the chest high desk and looked at me. Mark's shoulders remained tensed, probably because he hadn't actually stopped what he was doing but merely paused while he waited to see what I would ask of him. He looked a bit less nervous now that I was there. I wondered if Penn had been asking him the same sorts of questions.

"I have no idea." I stared at Penn, daring him to accuse my employee of murder. Not that there was much I could do if he did. I could, however, make sure that Jake had a good attorney.

Detective Granger came around the corner from the elevators.

She shook her head. "Not hiding in the office down there."

I found it annoying that she'd just taken it upon herself to head down. I hoped she hadn't frightened Brandon too much.

Granger looked at me. "I suppose you have a good story about this employee, too? You knew he had anger management issues, right?"

"I knew he'd been through treatment," I said. Now I was uncomfortable.

Mark's arms lowered slightly. He must have been resting his hands on the counter, which was lower on his side. The chest high counter was nearly chin high on Granger. She really was short.

She nodded, waiting.

I didn't know what else to say. No one knew I'd heard him arguing with Floyd. Well, I had told Suzanne but I couldn't imagine her saying something. I couldn't believe anyone else would have overheard them.

This had to be one of those times when detectives

hoped that their silence would make one of us talk. Fortunately, Suzanne was busy. Mark didn't know anything—at least I didn't think he did. I bit my tongue to keep myself from speaking.

Finally, Penn spoke. "We'll need to see him as soon as possible."

"I asked the young man at the reception area for another copy of the feeds," Granger said. She glared at me as she said it, as though I were the one who had refused to get them the video feeds and then turned and headed out.

"I had a thought," I called after her.

She turned to me. "You did?" There was a dry tone to her voice, as if she were surprised that I ever thought.

"What about Corbin Moore's children? Where are they? Obviously, he couldn't have murdered Floyd, but what if they just learned something about their father's death and now blame Floyd? It would explain why it happened so long after Moore's death. Floyd was killed on the anniversary of Moore's death."

Granger raised an eyebrow. "We're already looking into them."

Then she turned once more and marched out, moving quickly, like a hummingbird, probably so that I couldn't call out another idea. I wasn't sure what she thought of the one I had just called out. Her face had given nothing away.

"He had kids?" Mark asked.

I nodded.

"There's a Norman Moore staying on the second floor," Mark said. He looked something up. "He checked out this morning."

I raised an eyebrow. It gave me a name to start with. I'd check to be sure that any Norman Moores who might be staying here had nothing to do with Corbin Moore from Charlotte.

Moving around the desk so I could hide out in my office and not get as much done as I needed, I heard the main doors opening. It's one of those sounds I hardly notice but there was something off about the hurried feet after the door closed again. It made me turn.

Jake and Ari were practically running across the lobby.

Chapter Twenty-Four

I kept my jaw from hitting the floor, but only just, as I slowly put together a few pieces. Ari had been staying local. She was seeing someone younger, someone her family wouldn't approve of. Jake fit all those things. They weren't holding hands, but something about the way they were hurrying together, in step, easy with each other, suggested a deeper relationship than owner and hotel employee.

The lobby bar music changed to a quieter, slower tune, almost like a movie readying for a romantic scene. Of course, rather than the scent of hundreds of roses I smelled pizza, so that didn't quite complete the image.

"Jake," I said, waiting for him to cross the lobby.

"We were going to tell you," Ari said. "But…"

"But we were waiting. Except I had to," Jake went on.

He looked at Ari. She nodded.

"Ari is on the tape. She's not on the top floor, but she's in the lobby and then down in the basement. She didn't stay here…" Jake gulped and glanced over at her.

"I stayed with Jake," Ari finished. She straightened.

Her hair was colored black, though the lines on her face showed her age. She was still slim and whatever she wore under her designer clothing, she looked as firm as I had at forty, which is saying not perfect, but not sagging down to her knees, either.

Ari smiled again. There was something bright when she did that. Her eyes had a sparkle. I'd always thought Ari was an attractive woman and wondered why she wasn't married. It was surprising, however, that a young man like Jake found her attractive. He didn't seem her type. I would have imagined her with someone who loved art and opera or something. Jake was more outdoorsy.

"She didn't want anyone to know," Jake said. "We're waiting for her attorney to get here. The attorney arrived in Charlotte a few hours ago."

I nodded. "But you didn't want to take the chance that the video would get to the police before that."

"Right."

"You just missed Granger and Penn," I said.

"We saw them drive off." Ari glanced back lest the two suddenly return.

"I wanted to be sure you knew what was going on," Jake said. "I know I shouldn't date someone who works here, but Ari doesn't exactly work here?"

"Well, I'm not sure I can do anything about someone who is my boss," I told him. It wasn't exactly proper, but that was a problem for the Bowman family to work out.

"We only have each other as alibis," Ari said. "At least if the information I got from the police was accurate."

"Which they'll try to claim aren't good alibis at all."

Ari nodded. "They could try to place blame on both of us."

I crossed my arms. We really needed to find out who had killed Floyd. I had a feeling that Corbin's children might be a lead. First, though, I needed to make sure that Ari and Jake weren't found by the police. I didn't want my workers to have to lie if they were questioned. Mark and Suzanne had already seen us talking.

"Why don't you drive out towards Lyle's cabin?" I suggested. "You could say you were going for a little hike while waiting for Ari's attorney."

It was as good a story as I could come up with. And it would get them out of the Neary-Ten. Even if Mark and Suzanne felt they had to say something, at least they wouldn't necessarily know where the two went afterwards.

"And if the detectives find you first, remember to wait for Ari's attorney and anyone she can find to represent you, Jake," I looked pointedly at him and then at Ari, to make sure she knew I expected her to foot the bill for any legal representation he needed.

"They've already voiced concerns about Jake's anger management background."

Ari sighed. She got on her phone, but the two of them left. Mark wasn't behind me any longer, having gone to help Suzanne. Good. I didn't need to worry that he'd over-head anything and could tell the police I was helping to hide two people who seemed to be suspects in the murder. Even if it was only until their attorneys arrived.

Chapter Twenty-Five

My office felt like a sanctuary. I rarely closed the door but I did so just then, because I need to shut out any sounds of the police if they came back. It would allow me to avoid answering any knocks for a few more minutes, which might buy Ari and Jake time to meet their attorneys and head to the station. I knew they were both suspects but I didn't think either of them had harmed Floyd.

Thinking back to Jake's conversation with Floyd, Floyd had to have known who Ari's affair was with. He could easily have been following her. She thought he had some sort of tracker on her phone. If the tracker application was on Floyd's phone, it might have explained the detective saying she pinged Ari's phone. Perhaps they had used Floyd's tracking device. Generally speaking, it seemed like an unusual thing to do unless there was a reason to worry about her location, like they thought she might have been killed as well. So far as I knew, they had gotten in contact with her pretty easily.

Booting my computer, I listened to the whining of the hard drive, reminding me that I really needed a new system. This one was old. I didn't want to spend the money but if I didn't do so soon, I'd probably end up having to make do with a front counter computer for a few weeks while something was ordered. On a day like today, the idea of having to stand in front of people and pretend like nothing was going on felt overwhelming.

The office grew chilly, but Olive didn't immediately pop in. I hoped that wasn't a sign that Floyd was going to be haunting the hotel. I shuddered at the thought of him looking over my shoulder as I did my work. And well, perhaps a little bit from the cold.

It was hard to concentrate thinking that he might be there. Finally, Olive showed up. She shook her head.

"I was waiting to see what you were going to look up. I didn't want to interrupt." She fingered her pearls.

"When I didn't see you, I started worrying that the chill was from Floyd," I told her. "And that put me off doing anything much at all."

Olive made a face. "I hope he doesn't end up haunting the place. We'd be forever at each other's throats. Do you suppose that one ghost can banish another?"

"You're the expert," I reminded her.

"What have you learned?"

"Ari and Jake are a thing," I said.

Olive raised her eyebrows and then shrugged. "Everyone has to find someone."

"And I'm still wondering about Corbin Moore's children. I did point that out to Detective Granger. She and Detective Penn came by for the video Jake was going to give them but he wasn't in his office."

"I noted he and Ari left together. I shouldn't have been at all surprised when you said they were a thing, though it wasn't impossible that he was bringing her into the police. I can't imagine Ari as a murderer though."

"I can't imagine either of them. I mean, if Floyd had been hit or something, maybe I could see Jake, but not with a knife." I leaned back in my chair thinking about the whole mess.

Olive stood where she was staring off at my bookshelves, or perhaps into space. Maybe she could find other ghosts that way? I knew she was thinking.

"I don't know Jake that well but I knew Ari. Perhaps not well and, of course, I had a reason to be grateful to her. I can't see her with a murderer. She seemed very astute. Of all the Bowmans she seemed most aware of Floyd's shortcomings and she knew how to manage them, mostly. I mean, Floyd was never really manageable. I can see her getting tired of managing him, but I think she'd just have let the others see what sort of person Floyd actually was. That would have been a more satisfying end to him than murdering him, at least for her. I suspect she'd take exception to someone who could have murdered her brother, even if she often wanted to."

Interesting observations. I didn't know Ari well at all, but what I did know I liked. I suspected Olive was right about her managing Floyd for the rest of the family. There was no reason to suspect anything else.

"What have you found out about Corbin Moore's children?" Olive asked.

"Nothing, yet," I said. "I was just about to sit down and start searching when you didn't quite appear."

Olive gave me a look. She then just popped out. I sighed. The chill left and I knew she wasn't hovering invisibly over my shoulder. At least I didn't think she was. That would be something to find out, although I doubted Olive would actually tell me.

I started searching Norman Moore's name. I had an address thanks to his driver's license. I looked him up generally. There were photos of him with his mom and dad and none of them matched what I knew of Corbin Moore's family. No one named Corbin or Jean in the family. Not a relative then. It was doubtful he was a suspect.

I tried searching Corbin and Jean Moore together and this time I got a handful of hits. Unsurprisingly, one of them was the younger sister, Constance, who had died only a few years ago. Jean was still alive at the time of the obituary. She was named, but the children were just listed as assorted cousins and nieces and nephews in the write up.

That was unhelpful. There had to be a better way to go about finding out the names of the children. But nothing I put into the search engines was any help at all. I sighed and tried to focus on work. I wasn't any more successful then than I had been earlier.

In fact, I was less so. I hoped that Ari's attorney got to them soon and that she'd found someone good to represent Jake. I also hoped the fact that she was on a video leaving the hotel meant that the police would think she'd have known about those cameras and blocked them as well. Of course, Granger would push and push and push.

Suzanne knocked and poked her head into the office to let me know she was off. I knew she was headed downstairs to work with Olive on the novel. The two were working hard. I hoped that it brought in some income for Suzanne. It wasn't as if Olive had a bank account that she could pay Suzanne from. The bank account was one of the many things that would be difficult for Olive to manage without assistance. I hoped Suzanne knew what she was getting into.

I pushed myself up and went to see how things were going. Both Mark and the part-timer had someone in front of them checking in. No one waited in line. Most of our weekend guests had arrived the other day or had come in earlier while I was busy with Olive in my office. I slipped out the side door and decided to see if Jean was in her room.

I walked over to the elevator. I had thought about just riding up but then figured that it would be rude to just knock on the door. I picked up the black house phone that we still had on tables by the elevators. They were almost never used, but we kept them in case of an emergency.

I dialed the room number and it rang through. Jean answered on the third ring.

"Hello?"

"Jean?" I asked.

"Speaking."

"This is Maggie Davenport, the manager of the Neary-Ten. I was wondering if you'd mind chatting with me a bit about what you know about ghosts. I'm trying to learn more about the one in your room."

"I can do that. Do you want to meet me in the bar on the second floor, or is that the Mezzanine?"

"We call it the Mezzanine, but I know where you mean," I said.

"Give me about ten minutes," Jean told me, ringing off.

I left the area by the elevator, passing a heavyset woman dragging her bag behind her going the other direction. I gave her a smile and she nodded back at me.

Then I hurried up the main stairs to the mezzanine.

Soft jazz played up there. While louder pop music played in the lobby, once inside the bar, the two didn't combat each other nearly as much as I'd have thought when I first started at the hotel. You could actually hear the jazz music. Now and then a particularly heavy beat from downstairs might put a wrinkle in the softer music from above but it was a rare thing. I suspected that on Friday night when things were a bit more hopping downstairs it might happen more often, though even then we didn't get complaints.

"Maggie," Eliza said coming over with a menu.

I waved my hand at the menu. "Just a lemonade please," I said.

Eliza nodded at me. I was seated near the entrance. I could see out through the glass. In the far corner was the piano, but no one sat at it this early. Later, we'd have someone from town playing live music.

While quite a number of people were downstairs, there were only a handful up here. The bar was set back a bit and while people noticed the tables that sprawled out the door to oversee the lower level, not everyone noticed the darker, enclosed bar area. It seemed obvious to me, but I had been told on many guest surveys that people were disappointed that they hadn't noticed this area sooner.

In some ways that was good. It kept the place quieter while the wilder fun went on downstairs.

I sipped my lemonade and people watched. In exactly ten minutes Jean appeared in the doorway. She was dressed in capris and a red and pink floral cotton shirt with short flowing sleeves. She smiled upon seeing me and headed over before Eliza could ask her if she wanted a table.

"It's lovely to have someone to talk to for a while. I adore the spa, of course, but hauntings are a passion of mine," she said.

Eliza came over and took Jean's order. I wasn't surprised when she ordered a white wine after questioning Eliza quite thoroughly on the offerings. Jean seemed like a wine lover.

"I don't know much about hauntings, other than what I've picked up in relation to the hotel. I mostly went with the theme because I thought of it as a marketing tool. I think I might need to know more if I want to know more about the ghost in your suite," I said after Jean had gotten her drink.

The wine smelled like wine to me, though Jean took a long whiff and swirled the pale liquid in her glass and smiled approvingly.

"I'm not an expert," Jean acknowledged. "I lost my parents when I was young and I always wanted to contact them on the other side."

I sipped my lemonade, the sugary lemon keeping me from having to make a comment. Fortunately, Jean was not the sort to sit and wait for a comment.

"I was so young then and didn't know any better," she went on. "Now I do. Mostly spirits come if they want to or if there's a reason. My parents had no real reason to appear. I liked to think that they were watching over me but they weren't willing to chat, so to speak. But it gave me a basis for my later fascination. I tried again when my husband died, but still, I can't say that I learned all that much. I think I've learned more here, seeing a ghost myself, than I have in all that time."

I nodded. I could understand.

"Anyway, I started reading and one of the things I've done is visit the little paranormal museums around the country. Some of them are silly. Some are interesting. I learned more than I need to know about Bigfoot, who seems to end up in those museums as often as ghosts, but I also learned about ghosts and ghost hunting."

"We've had a few ghost hunting conferences here," I said. "I find the hunters quite passionate about their hobby."

"Isn't it true of any hobby?" Jean asked. "But I think when you hunt ghosts, you're used to being an outsider of sorts so it becomes more about your identity."

That was something I hadn't thought of, but she was probably right. Many of the people at those conferences tended to be somewhat socially awkward. Not shy or rude, just awkward about meeting people.

She sipped her wine and smiled a little.

"I haven't seen the ghost in the room again. The fact that he died on that day makes me think that's why he shows up then. But he didn't die in the room, you said." Jean watched me for a moment, perhaps hoping for more information.

I reiterated the car accident.

"It wasn't made to look like he was in the car?" she asked.

"Not to my knowledge. In fact, I think people said his wife left earlier and he had checked out to head home. In those days, you had to go to the desk."

"The killer could have impersonated him," Jean argued.

I cocked my head. It would have had to go on a credit card but perhaps they didn't check identification with the credit card then. I wasn't there to know one way or another.

"Or maybe the room is the last thing he remembered. Did the wife plan to leave earlier or was there something else?" Jean probed me for information.

"I heard there was a domestic altercation around here and then she left," I said.

"He may have been shocked that she left, so the room is the last place he remembers," Jean said. "How very sad." She seemed did seem quite sorrowful that such a thing had happened.

I agreed.

"Could he show up when his killer was around the hotel?" I didn't want to suggest that Floyd had done it. I mean, no need to air dirty laundry with a guest. Bad enough that I was asking her for her opinion.

"I wouldn't be surprised if a ghost did that. Or perhaps someone related to him arrived. He certainly didn't look like anyone I knew, but perhaps there's someone else in the hotel?" Jean watched me carefully.

"I've looked through the guest records and it doesn't seem like there was anyone with his last name. I haven't gotten far on locating his family."

"If the wife left him, she may have remarried," Jean said carefully.

I raised an eyebrow. Possible. But there was no way I was going to be able to find that out. I hoped that Granger and Penn would have better luck than I was having. I mean, Corbin's wife was named Jean, and I was talking to Jean so it could be her, but then she'd have said, surely.

"There's so many variables in searching out a ghost, aren't there?" Jean was sympathetic. "I think that's what I love, though. It's the ultimate murder mystery."

Jean looked away, her cheeks slightly reddened. Perhaps she thought that she'd said something in poor taste. After all, we did just have a murder here. Maybe she thought we all actually liked Floyd.

"It was nice that we at least got a name for the ghost," I said. "He seemed awfully friendly. I mean, for a ghost."

Jean chuckled. "I haven't ever talked to a ghost before, but you were just right there talking to him as if you did it all the time."

I was tempted to tell her I actually did, only not to him. I didn't want to out Olive. While it was clear she was a ghost to those of us who knew her, those in the hotel who hadn't yet realized it, didn't need to know. Olive did take great pleasure in seeing who noticed that she didn't actually walk and how many people never even gave her a second look.

Jean and I sipped our drinks, talking a bit more about ghosts, but she had no real insights into how I could find out more about Corbin Moore, not unless I found someone who had known him. Unfortunately, finding a name of anyone who had known him was my problem.

Chapter Twenty-Six

Later that evening, I headed down to my apartment to settle in, have some dinner, and actually spend time with my cats. Latte and Chai had been neglected the last few days. While I'd been there to feed them and spent some time down there, I had been out of my usual routine. All cats hated it when routines were disrupted, and Siamese could be particularly sensitive.

Fortunately for the boys, I, too, was a creature of habit and I didn't often break up the routine for them. When I did, it tended to be something that had been out of my control. Rather like someone murdering Floyd.

The dishes from my dinner had been put in the dishwasher and the room smelled like the savory tomato and basil soup that had made up the main course. I had the television on, though I wasn't really watching anything. It was a repeat of an old mystery show that I had liked. Tonight, though, my mind was spinning about the murder.

I absently played with one of the cats' favorite wand toys. It had a colorful feather on the end and I was pulling it around on the floor or swinging it around to create a fluttering sound that drove Chai mad. They'd take turns leaping for it or grabbing at if it were on the floor. They particularly liked it when it flipped up over the rug that lay in front of my wooden coffee table.

My phone rang startling all of us. Latte glared as if I were somehow to blame. I suppose he wasn't exactly wrong even if I hadn't been the one to call. Chai gave a long suffering huff, which was the feline equivalent of a sigh. His play time was going to be interrupted even if I didn't end up leaving.

"This is Maggie," I answered.

"It's Addy," my front desk person said. "I think you need to come up here. There's a police officer asking for information that I'm not sure about giving out."

I didn't ask her what it was.

"I'll be up in a couple of minutes. I need to find some shoes," I said. I hadn't changed clothes. I often do, particularly if I've worn a skirt. The last few days, I'd just worn trousers and a nice blouse which were comfortable enough to relax in at home. I wasn't one of those people who immediately changed into sweat pants and then had to completely dress before going out. Even when I did change out of a skirt, I tended to put on nice jeans.

All my shoes were flats that allowed me to do a lot of walking if I needed to. You never knew what a manager might be called to do. They were all, also, black. I had flats that went with skirts, with trousers and my trusty tennis shoes, which were the best. I put those on because I was not going to have Detective Granger thinking I was just sitting around waiting for her.

"Sorry boys," I said to the cats and headed up the stairs. I purposely didn't hurry. I couldn't image that there was anyone in the hotel that was dangerous. If a guest had murdered Floyd, they had to think they were either in the clear or they had left. It would be up to the detectives to track those people down.

As for my employees, I couldn't imagine any of them murdering someone. I hardly knew Ryan, but I trusted Teri, his boss. If she didn't think he'd done something, then I was willing to take her at her word, at least until someone showed me proof otherwise.

The hallway got cold. For a moment I dared hope that Olive would show up, but it was just Clara running towards me. I was close enough to the stairs that I didn't get quite the same level of iciness that I might have had she run right next to me. I nodded at her, though she never really seemed to see me. However, earlier in the year, Olive said she'd asked Clara to provide a distraction, and the ghost had definitely winked at me when I saw her running down the hall. Because of that, I had a feeling Clara knew more than I'd always given her credit for.

The stair second from the bottom squeaked when I placed my foot on it. It had been a problem from the day I started, though sometimes when other work was being done, I'd have the handyman take a look and see if it was fixable. They always said it was and then it would be good for a few months. The last worker had managed a good seven months which was probably a record.

Music floated down from the lobby bar. The smell of French fries was nearly overwhelming and suddenly made my tomato soup dinner seem rather puny. My stomach, which had been pleasantly pleased just moments ago, took that second to growl in annoyance at not getting something more substantial.

No help for it. I wasn't going to go in there and order something. They were busy.

Detective Granger stood near the front desk. Addy, my night manger wasn't particularly tall but even she was taller than the detective. Fortunately, the people in the lobby were all interested in their own lives and not paying attention to the fact that the police were here, *again*.

"Can I help you?" I asked reaching the desk.

"I need access to all the information on your head of security. Personnel records, whatever information you have. I also need to know what he's been working on." Granger handed me a paper. It was a broad warrant, but because Jake worked in security, I understood why Addy had been reluctant.

"Pull up personnel records and print them," I told Addy.

"Already working on it," Addy said.

Listening a bit more closely, I heard the printer in the little alcove next to my office whirring away like a whisper in the background. No wonder I hadn't noticed.

I sighed at some of the other information.

"I don't know exactly what Jake was working on, as you put it," I said. "He's my head of security."

Granger stared at me. "You admit that you don't know what your employees are up to."

"Have you found him?" I asked.

Granger stared at me, perhaps trying to assess how much I already knew and if she could accuse me of perhaps hindering her investigation. I kept my face neutral.

"I just need files on anything he was working on," Granger said.

"I'll send you down to our security department. Mostly, today, he was working on downloading those videos. And probably next week's personnel schedule."

"He doesn't walk the hotel?"

"All our security people walk the hotel. Unless there's something amiss, there aren't really any reports."

"I want to see those," she said.

I nodded. I called down and let the young woman on the desk know that Granger was on her way down and that she should cooperate with the detective. Then I placed a call to the hotel's attorney to let them know what was happening. I scanned the document copy that Granger had left me with into the system and sent it off. If there were problems, they could sort them out.

Sighing I looked around. The people over by the bar looked like they were having fun. I'd just treated myself to a drink last night. I wondered if I dared do so again.

"Go for it," Addy said, practically reading my mind.

"Do I look like I need it that much?" I asked.

She nodded. "It's been stressful around here. I can't imagine Jake doing something to Floyd, no matter that he was sneaking around with Ari."

"You knew?" I asked.

"She usually waits for Jake out in the parking lot when she picks him up, maybe once a month or so. We never have help at the doors that late so once I went out to make sure she didn't need anything. She said no and turned away like she didn't want to be recognized. I pretended I didn't know who she was, even though I did. Her face is all over the employee newsletters we get," Addy said.

"I just found out."

"This happened about a year ago so it's been going on for at least that long. I got the impression that the relationship wasn't new," Addy said.

Interesting.

"Any insight into Floyd's murder?" I asked.

"Unfortunately, no. No one snuck down looking suspicious that night or I'd have said something. It's just weird though. That poor woman who knew something, but never got a chance to share."

"I know. I feel badly for her."

"Jake didn't do it. He and Ari weren't here that night," Addy said. "I saw them leave together. Floyd was watching from the bar and then he went upstairs. He was whistling like he knew something when he walked by here."

"You told the detectives this?"

Addy nodded. "Not that it helped. But Granger did want to know what he was whistling as if that made a difference."

I chuckled. I couldn't imagine it did.

But my talk with Addy had given me time to give myself permission to head over to the bar and have a drink.

Chapter Twenty-Seven

The bar was crowded enough that there were no tables free. There was a single seat near the bar itself and I slipped through the people talking and sometimes singing to get to it. This was the first really lovely weekend we'd had this summer. People were out and about and it was just late enough that most were looking for a way to recoup after their adventures. That sort of timing was always good for the Neary-Ten.

Teri and Ryan were behind the bar. Ryan glanced at me, but turned away. Teri came over from her spot, though it looked like she'd been working the other end of the bar, and asked what I wanted.

"Do you do the white wine sangria or is that just upstairs?" I asked.

"Just upstairs, unfortunately," Teri said. "I have regular sangria if you'd like?"

"Sure." I wasn't particularly picky. I could have walked upstairs and gotten exactly what I wanted, but once I had pushed myself up on the stool, I didn't want to move again. The fries smelled good and the music, while too loud for my taste, had a nice beat. It perked up my mood after what had been going on with the murder.

I noted Ryan making the drink but he gave it to Teri to bring down to me.

"Is there a problem with Ryan?" I asked.

"I think he's intimidated," Teri said. "The police were back asking questions this afternoon. They left, but I think he feels as if everyone thinks he did it, no matter what I say. He made a comment about you coming here to keep an eye on him."

I shook my head. "That's not it at all. I'm just stressed. Granger is looking into Jake. I know he didn't do it. Addy can vouch for seeing him leave, too."

"Right?" Teri said. "It has to be a guest. They've probably already cleared out."

I agreed that that was the most likely. I hated the idea that I was making Ryan uncomfortable. I left a tip and slipped out of the bar to take my drink somewhere else.

Through the main doors I noticed that the sunset was a perfectly lovely orange and red. I decided to take my drink down towards the spa. There was a little patio that few people knew about in that direction. I could enjoy my drink and have a bit of time to think. My cats were already unhappy with me. It wouldn't hurt if I took a bit of me-time to try and unwind. Surely, they didn't want me over-stressed either.

The patio was a small area located outside the hallway that connected the spa wing to the original part of the hotel. The way the building had angled, the builders of the addition decided to create a little outdoor area. Perhaps someone had considered having a bar down at that end but it had never come about. The hallway ran along the windowed side to the spa, with a large conference room off to the other side. The conference rooms had the better view, looking out over the low hills. The hallway view was of a few trees and our parking lot, which, happily, was quite full.

The blue and green speckled carpet lined the hallway floors, a little more worn than that on most of the room floors. We got a lot of traffic back and forth to the spa. Even locals who used the spa often came in through the main doors and then walked down to where they needed to be, though there were doors to the spa itself just beyond the patio where I intended to relax.

The patio had a view of the parking lot, but beyond the lot and off to the side were the tall trees of the area, a mix of deciduous trees that dropped their leaves in gorgeous color in the fall, and evergreens. The latter tended to be scraggly compared to those I remembered from my home in the northwest. The other trees, though, more than made up for it in the variety of shapes and sizes.

The scent of pine and forest mingled with the salty clean smell of the spa, giving the little space a pleasant enough aroma. The chairs were large, cushioned patio chairs, the cushions pulled in for the winter but put out again daily, unless it was pouring rain. Everything was waterproof.

The dark fake rattan of the chairs mingled nicely with the pale stone of the patio. There were six chairs with a small table between every two. No one else was out there, though I wasn't surprised.

The pink and red sunset was gorgeous. I knew that the most gorgeous sunsets often foretold clouds coming in. Tomorrow probably wouldn't be as nice as the last few days, which was unfortunate. I sipped my sangria, letting the alcohol warm my blood and my body.

A breeze whispered through the trees and ruffled my hair. It cool but not unpleasantly so. I needed to remember to get outside more. I walked back and forth inside the hotel all the time. I tried to make sure I spent at least a little time outside every day, but with the upheaval of Floyd's murder, I'd been stuck inside for nearly three days.

It was too bad any rain that was supposed to fall hadn't happened while I was too busy to think about more than the occasional short trip over to the restaurant to check in on something. At least I'd remembered to relax now.

When I had been new to the Neary-Ten, my then boss, Olive, had shown me this little space. She'd loved it.

"It's the best part of this overbuilding. The owners are hanging on, but I'm not sure for how much longer," she'd said. She'd looked around, appearing sad at the thought of not working there if the hotel was sold and perhaps closed.

Hang on we had and after Olive had died and I started seeing her ghost all the time, I'd decided to market the hotel as haunted. It had taken a bit of time, but it had more than worked out. The Bowmans had been pleased. Floyd, perhaps, less so than others. If the idea had been his, he'd have been pleased, but he didn't like to think that someone else could have a good idea. Or maybe it was that I was woman with a good marketing idea, though I suspected he was an equal opportunity hater.

I heard someone come through the door behind me. There was the slightest squeak.

I glanced back.

Ryan was still in his apron and was rubbing his hands on it.

"Oh hello," I said. "I'd have brought my glass back, if that's what you're worried about."

He shook his head looking around at the patio.

"I like it out here sometimes. It's quiet," he said. He walked over to the chair near mine. He didn't sit. He leaned a knee on it, though. His black jeans were worn.

Even the edges of the long-sleeve shirt he wore were slightly frayed, though not badly.

"It is," I agreed. I wasn't quite ready to get up and go back inside but it bothered me that he was out there when I'd wanted to be alone with my thoughts. I wanted to think about what might have happened to Floyd and to Wendy.

"Were you checking out my work? Did Floyd tell you I wasn't a good worker?" Ryan asked.

"I was having a glass of sangria," I said. "It's been a stressful few days and I thought it would help me unwind." Perhaps he'd catch on that he wasn't helping.

"But you think that I could have stolen from the bar?" Ryan pressed.

I made myself remain still. I had my cell phone. I could call for help if I needed it. There were cameras in the corners of the patio. The spa was closed, but I doubted everyone had gone home yet. If I yelled, someone would hear. Security might even see that I was uncomfortable.

"Floyd didn't like my father, either," Ryan said.

"I didn't know your family knew his," I said.

"A little," Ryan said. "My dad was a banker."

A slight chill went through me. Ryan's last name wasn't Moore but it reminded me of what Jean had said. That names could change.

"Really?" I asked. I didn't gulp. Instead, I took a sip of the sangria, as if I didn't have a care in the world.

I had one hand in my pocket and fumbled with my phone. I wanted to text but didn't know if I could press the buttons to do so. I couldn't even accidentally call someone like Lyle because, chances were, the phone was locked. We had all this technology that was supposed to help make us safer but if you couldn't get to it, it didn't help at all.

The door opened behind us. I glanced over. So did Ryan. Jean was still dressed in the outfit she'd had on earlier. There was a bit more color in her cheeks. She frowned upon seeing us.

"What are you doing, Ryan?" she asked. She stepped close to the chair where Ryan stood.

Her last name wasn't Phillips. I had no idea the two even knew each other.

"Mom..." Ryan started and then looked away.

Jean frowned. "You didn't?"

"Who else was going to?" Ryan asked, tensing his body. "It's the whole reason I've been working on getting jobs in the places he worked."

"That man did us a favor!" Jean snapped. "What have you done?"

Ryan's hand flashed from beneath the apron he wore. A large knife, flashed, the black handle with the sliver line on the edge signaling it was from the kitchen in the bar.

Jean gasped and leaned back as it slashed towards her neck.

Her hand went up as she stumbled back. Blood flowed but not as much as if Ryan had hit an artery. She had a chance.

I didn't hesitate to pull out my phone and start punching in 911. That didn't require my phone to be unlocked, thankfully.

I'd barely started talking when Ryan pulled the phone from my hand and hung up, tossing it away.

The knife was down at his side. I took that moment to move out of reach. I didn't want to have my throat slashed. Jean was sitting with her back to the windows of the hallway. I hoped that someone from security would be watching. Even if they weren't, perhaps someone would be doing a walk-through.

"No one can see us," Ryan said. He didn't move

towards me, but the knife, now edged with red from Jean's neck, was still out, wavering slightly.

"No. There's no one here." I had to agree with that. While we could see the parking lot, it was the side. People didn't normally come all the way over to this edge to drive around, not unless the lot was really full. Even then, most were looking for parking nearer the restaurant at this time of day.

It was also late enough and cool enough that I couldn't count on the bell person to be waiting outside to assist guests. They might be in the lobby staying warmer. Some of them liked the cool air in the evening. Other times they liked the inside or even the air lock that let people into the main lobby.

"When Teri told me where you were going, I made sure to turn this camera off," Ryan said. "I took computer classes so I could make my way around the hotel and not have people spying."

That creeped me out. I wondered if he'd gone in other rooms where he had no right to be.

"I had to make sure that when the Bowman's came here, I could get to them," he said.

"Why the Bowmans?" I asked. I could understand Floyd.

"They wanted the loan from my dad's bank. When he couldn't offer it to them, the young one, that Floyd, killed him. Everyone thought it was a car accident and she," at this point, Ryan gestured to Jean, "was happy to play along, but I knew it was purposeful. He even admitted it before I killed him."

Ryan seemed pleased.

Maybe, after everything that had gone on, security would come to check out the area where the camera was glitching. Jake would have made sure someone did it.

Unfortunately, Jake was probably at the police station talking to Detective Granger.

"Why kill the woman next door?" I asked.

"She complained," Ryan said. "I wasn't quite done with him, but she complained so everyone knew about his death too soon. I'd even seen the Bowman sister around and had hoped that maybe she would go up and visit and find him. Then I could take her out as well."

"Ari didn't even know Floyd was here," I said. "And Ari would never have murdered your father. It's not wrong to seek out a loan."

"Yeah?!" Ryan raised his voice. I hoped that it was loud enough to carry across the parking lot or maybe into the spa.

"You'd be wrong. You're too stupid to understand," he snapped. "Denying that loan was what got my father murdered. That and her—" again the gesture towards Jean — "leaving sooner. She probably had the hots for Floyd."

Ryan was edging closer, using the knife to point towards Jean. He'd wave it around when he did so, as if trying to figure out where to use it to best effect. She was still sitting up but she didn't look good. I hoped it was just shock and not blood loss. While there was blood running down her front, it didn't look to be so much that she would die from it.

I noticed a phone in her hand as well. I looked away, not wanting to stare, to give away my hopes that she was calling for help. Or at least texting help.

My movements distracted Ryan and he took a step towards me. I stepped back towards the edge of the patio. We had holly growing around the edges and some low plants that had their own sticky leaves. If I leaped through there my pants would be shredded and my legs would hurt. It was the only way out, though. There was one spot where there was a narrow place that I could try and slip through to the parking lot.

Then maybe I could run fast enough to get away.

"I wouldn't try it," Ryan said. "I used to run track."

I looked at his long legs. He was taller than I was, probably faster. He was younger, too, by at least a decade, perhaps more.

"Why do you and your mom have different last names?" I asked.

"She was a whore, marrying around. One of them adopted me, but she got rid of him, too," Ryan sneered. "She was always a liar."

I said nothing. I liked Jean. I hoped that she'd be okay. I wondered, though, if she had known that Floyd would be there, or if her arriving was just a coincidence. Maybe she wanted to commemorate the death of her husband.

A few pieces slid into place. Maybe the reason Floyd was at the hotel had nothing to do with Ari. Maybe that was a coincidence. Maybe Ryan had set something up and Floyd had come there to meet someone. I recalled what Suzanne said about a phone call.

"Did you set Floyd up to arrive on the anniversary of your father's death?" I asked quietly.

Ryan smiled at me. "You aren't completely stupid."

"How?" I asked. I took another small step, basically slipping back, hoping he wouldn't notice I was further away.

"I told him I knew what he'd done to my father and that I had proof. He needed to pay me cash or I'd turn him in," Ryan said. "It was a win-win."

Floyd would have turned that down. The death was so many years ago that no doubt he figured there would be enough questions that he'd never be convicted. Even if Floyd had been found holding a murder weapon and filmed, he had the sort of ego that would have made him think he'd never be convicted even then.

"And he refused," Ryan went on. Not surprised.

"Which is when you killed him," I said.

"Wasn't meant to. But then he started going on about how he had me on stealing liquor from the hotel, which was bunk. Floyd said it wouldn't matter because you'd have to listen to him or he'd have your job. I did it for you!"

I tried sliding back another step, but the knife was once again in my face, Ryan waving it around, getting closer.

"But you kept coming in, sticking your nose in, testing me, to be sure I wasn't stealing!" Ryan had raised his voice this time.

I heard a car in the parking lot but my back was to it so I couldn't see if maybe it was the police.

Ryan took another step.

No one was coming, or if they were, they weren't coming in time.

I breathed in and out, trying to calm my body. Not for death, of course. I didn't want to die. I most certainly didn't want to die in the Neary-Ten and perhaps end up a ghost hanging out with Olive talking about whatever ghosts spoke about when the living weren't around. Besides, my cats needed me.

The martial arts courses I'd been taking had taught me to use my attacker's body against them. I watched the way Ryan moved. When he sliced the knife towards me, I slipped sideways instead of back, coming closer to him.

As a smaller, older woman, I didn't have the upper body strength to take him on, but I was able to deliver a good swift kick to his groin.

Ryan doubled over, squeaking out a few choice words as I slipped around him.

Instead of shredding myself on the holly, I ran for the

door to the hallway of the hotel. Although he was still doubled over, he reached out snagging my pants.

The air got icy cold, like Olive was there. I didn't know what she'd do to help. I had to make the hallway. People would be there. I could scream and someone would come running.

Ryan's fingers let go. As I stumbled forward towards the doors, I saw the ghost that was Corbin Moore. He looked particularly sad. He shook his head looking at Ryan.

"It was an accident, son. Just an accident. I was mad. I was always mad in those days. Let them go…"

I didn't pause to listen to anything more. I flung the door open and ran as fast as I could down the carpeted hallway. I wished then that I had left the hallway as tile or hardwood, where my footsteps might have made some noise, to draw people to me.

My breath came too hard to scream. I thought I heard someone behind me but I had to keep going, to get help. Jean needed me. Chai and Latte needed me.

The hall was longer than I remembered. It had taken me barely any time at all when I'd gone to sit down and have a drink and relax. Now, though, it might have been part of a nightmare where nothing ended, but I needed to keep going.

Martial arts aside, I was not in great condition and I quickly picked up a stitch in my side.

I felt someone behind me more than heard them and I whipped to my left, slowing.

Ryan passed me, practically doubled over but still running.

"Fire!" I screamed with all the breath I could.

I'd learned long ago that if I were ever attacked to yell fire rather than help because people would come out to see a fire even if they weren't willing to help someone yelling for it.

Ryan turned faster than I had expected and quickly advanced on me.

I could only hope that someone in the lobby had heard me and came to my rescue. The knife in his hand looked very sharp.

Chapter Twenty-Eight

Time slows when you're facing potential death. It had happened before. I noted the way the right sleeve of Ryan's shirt had a long thread hanging from it. I smelled traces of beer on him, probably from letting foam flow over the glass on the tap beers. His breath came too fast and that smelled faintly of garlic and fish.

The carpet was soft under my foot, almost too soft for my expectation and I nearly threw myself off balance as I stepped back. I couldn't out run him again. I'd have to turn or I'd have to stumble backwards.

He rushed at me and I stepped to the side and then tried to run back down the hallway.

My chest hurt. It made me worry that I hadn't been able to yell loud enough.

But no sooner had I started my sprint when two security people and a bellhop all came running towards me. The girl in the bellhop vest was carrying a fire extinguisher with her. She'd moved to help in the smartest way possible.

My security people weren't armed unless they knew the

situation could escalate, in which case they carried batons or tasers. One of these two had brought a baton but the other carried one of our emergency blankets which was open, perhaps to wrap up someone who was on fire.

The woman with the baton held it up in a defensive position. I passed them but Ryan was no longer behind me. Looking back, he'd paused seeing other people.

"One of our guests is out on the patio. She's injured. If it hasn't been done so, we need to call 911," I gasped. I was still trying to catch my breath.

My heart was beating far too fast and I'd just nearly been killed. Had the three of them come around that corner any later and they might have found me bleeding on the floor while Ryan ran the other way.

The unarmed security guard was the red-haired man who had been at the reception desk the other day. He quickly pulled out a cell phone and started speaking a few seconds later, his voice not cracking, nor was he gasping for air between words like I would have been had I had my phone. Sadly, my own phone was back on the patio, probably broken.

Ryan had gone back out through that door. I worried for Jean. I stepped forward. I would have followed, to make sure he wasn't harming her, but the red-haired guard put an arm out to stop me.

"We have to help the guest," I gasped again, although what I expected them to do, I didn't know. My security had been trained to protect people and to do what they could to contain the situation until the police could get there. They weren't paid to be put in serious danger.

Moments later I heard sirens rushing towards us. It was too early for security's call to have drawn the police. Jean must have texted them successfully. I hoped she was still alive.

A burly looking man in a t-shirt and jeans came around the corner and stopped, frowning.

"What's going on?" he asked, puzzled.

"Please remain away from this hallway, sir," my female security guard told him. "There's nothing to worry about."

"Can I help?" he asked. From his build, he was probably a good guy to have in a fight.

"No sir," I said. "Just remain inside. And if you see the police send them this way."

Normally I'd have asked the bellhop to do it, but she was still holding the fire extinguisher up as if it were a weapon she was waiting to use. It wouldn't be such a bad one if the movies I'd been known to watch were any indication.

As the man moved away and towards the front doors, my female security guard edged down the hallway. She walked quickly towards the doors but slowed as she got there. She paused.

I watched as she opened the door carefully, the baton still at the ready. Then she leaned back and nodded at the other guard. All of my security people had to go through a basic first aid class. Jean would need more than that, but perhaps they could help enough to make sure she would make it to the hospital.

I followed slowly, not because I was tired but because I half-expected Ryan to jump out of a shadow at any moment. I thought I'd seen him go outside but maybe I had been wrong. It was strange how our minds tended to work after a scare like the one I'd had.

My hands felt shaky. I really needed to sit down. And probably have some hot decaffeinated tea and maybe a cookie to calm me down. But first I needed to know Jean was safe.

I heard someone running down the hall behind me. I turned.

Lyle was rushing down towards me.

"Maggie! I heard the call come through…"

I started to cry while I tried to tell him about Jean.

Lyle pulled me into a hug. I smelled the fresh pine scent of his shirt and the slightly musky masculine scent that was unabashedly Lyle. I would have loved to stay there and cry it out but Jean needed help.

"Jean," I said and pointed, not able to get the words out.

To his credit, Lyle let go and hurried off. I wasn't sure if that was a good thing for me or not. I mean, I wanted him to help Jean. But I also wanted comfort.

The hallway got cool and I shivered.

Olive popped in and stared at me. I could almost see her cataloging the streaks of tears down my cheeks and the mess of my hair. As I wiped a tear from the corner of my eye, my hands visibly did shake.

"Suzanne said something was going on." Olive made that a statement and not a question.

"It was Ryan," I blurted out.

"What was Ryan?" Olive asked. She looked over her shoulder. I heard people moving around the side of the building. More than just Lyle and the security guard.

Looking towards the lobby, I noticed the bellhop had left. She probably directed the first responders around the outside of the building. It would be faster, although they'd have to push through the holly bushes I'd avoided.

"Ryan murdered Floyd and Wendy," I told her. "And he tried to kill Jean."

"Who is Jean?" Olive asked. She was no longer in her concerned ghost mode. She was back to her imperious mode of looking down her nose at me. Seeing I hadn't related that I'd been knifed or had to fight off a man with a knife, she apparently thought I was fine and just having an emotional breakdown, something she'd never admit to having had.

"Jean was the woman in 785," I said.

Olive waited.

"She was married to Corbin Moore. Ryan was their son."

"Her last name was Moore and you didn't tell me?" Olive asked, looking at me as if I had committed a sin worse than murdering someone.

"It's not Moore. She remarried several times. I guess Ryan was adopted by one of the men but not her latest husband so they don't even share a last name," I said.

"Multiple husbands…Well, women who make bad choices often do so more than once. It's why I never wanted to get remarried or even involved with another man." Olive gave me a long look as if isolating herself was the best thing she could have done.

I didn't point out that in so doing she'd devoted her life to a hotel that she'd ended up haunting. Perhaps her mistake was my lesson and not hers.

"He tried to kill me, too, but I used the martial art moves that I learned to avoid the knife and kick him in the groin. And then Corbin Moore appeared and distracted him a little" I told her. Oddly, I wanted Olive's approval.

"That's rather crass, isn't it? But effective, I'm sure." Olive glided down the hallway to see what was going on.

Someone opened the door to the patio and I heard plenty of voices. The cavalry had arrived. I walked further down the hall to see that there were a couple of paramedics working over Jean. While she was being bandaged, she still appeared to be conscious. I hoped that was a good sign.

I went back out to thank the bellhop for thinking to send the responders around the outside. No need to have them parading through the lobby and getting the guests all up in arms.

Chapter Twenty-Nine

The weekend passed with the detectives questioning me again and figuring out what had happened. Given all the time they took and how behind I was, I didn't get any time off, although I made time for my martial arts class. It had probably saved my life. I was bound and determined to continue.

By Wednesday evening, things had settled down. Ryan had long since been caught hiding near the edge of the parking lot and was being held at the local police station and I had heard rumors he'd be pleading guilty. Olive insisted I join her and Suzanne in the Mezzanine Bar, though I wasn't sure what Olive was doing up there.

I left the main lobby, brightly lit against the thunderstorm that was drumming down outside and entered the darkened bar.

Our pianist played soft jazz over in the corner. The lights were dim and the room had the soft air of a quiet night. Guests who had only stayed the weekend had left so there were only a handful enjoying the ambiance. Suzanne sat at a table in a corner apart from the piano. She had a soda in front of her, though I didn't know if it had alcohol in it or not.

A plate of nachos was in the center of the table. The nachos were designed to share with four people so there was more than enough for us to make a hearty meal out of it if we wanted to. I wondered what was going on.

The smells of beer and fried foods swirled around, and that unique smell that would have told me I was in the Neary-Ten even if I were blindfolded pressed against me.

I settled into another one of the seats. Olive folded herself into a position that looked as if she, too, were sitting at the table.

"We have news," Olive said.

I raised an eyebrow.

"We've finished my book!"

"Congratulations!" I really was happy for them. I hoped the book did well enough that the two of them would profit from their work.

"We have a little problem," Suzanne said. "I put Olive's name on the book but said it was a pen name. But we'd like to use a photo of you, if that's okay. Her main character is a bit older than you and she uses terms Olive would use. It's hard for people to see someone my age talking like that, so we thought maybe you wouldn't mind if we used your image?"

I cocked my head. "I guess that would be okay. But I don't know what the book is about so it does need to be you who answers questions and stuff."

Suzanne nodded. "I can do that."

"We might want you to go to conferences," Olive told me.

I started to shake my head. The server came over and asked what I wanted. I had planned on having another drink but I'd had plenty in the last few days and this sounded like the sort of conversation where I wanted to have my wits about me. I ordered a lemonade.

"It won't be hard," Olive said. "And it would get you out of here. Make you more interesting."

"I'm just fine as I am," I said. I mean, this wasn't the first meal I'd had with Suzanne. Nor was I bound to the hotel. I had friends, younger friends, admittedly, in the martial arts class. Lyle called regularly. In fact, he'd been almost a pest making sure I was okay after Ryan had been arrested.

"You need to get out more," Olive said. "When was the last time you traveled anywhere?"

"While I love working at the Neary-Ten, I hate traveling on my own," I protested. "That's why I send Mark to conferences unless I really need to be there."

Olive shook her head as if that was a foolish thing.

"Even Jake has a girlfriend, if Ari can be called a girl," Olive said.

"And it nearly got him arrested." I mean, it wasn't bad that Ari and Jake were dating if that's what you called it at our age, but it had nearly gotten both of them arrested. Detective Granger had still been questioning Jake when the call had come in about Ryan. She hadn't dropped every-thing to find out what was happening, leaving that to Detective Penn.

Jake had cooled his heels in the station for two hours after Ryan had been arrested.

"You don't have to go that far, but it might help me create more realistic mysteries," Olive protested. "I can't go anywhere to set them in places I haven't been, but you could take pictures and describe things for me."

I glared. I was not going to be Olive's detective.

"I think," Suzanne broke in trying to be tactful, "that we have enough real excitement here."

I took a chip from the nachos while Suzanne scooped a few more for her little plate and ate a couple. Olive glared at the two of us, waiting until we could speak again. I knew she wanted me to just agree with her but I wasn't going to. I had my cats. And I had my friends in town and at the hotel. I had my sister, though she was out west.

"Why exactly was Ryan's last name different from Jean's?" Suzanne asked.

"The man she married after Corbin died had the last name Phillips. When they divorced, she remarried a third time," I said. "She told me that husband died a few years ago."

Olive nodded a long at that. "It's just as I said."

"Of course it is," I said, perhaps a bit too flippantly.

Olive pursed her lips but didn't say anything. I had a feeling if she did speak, she would have said something less than kind. Before her willpower broke, Suzanne broke in.

"When does she go home from the hospital?"

"She'll be discharged later this week. I'm planning on driving over to the hospital tomorrow afternoon." I glared at Olive. "I guess I *am* getting out."

"Do take notes on what the hospital looks like," Olive said. "And Suzanne talked about smells and sounds. Perhaps you could record something while you're there so I can hear the sounds."

I sighed. I was not getting out of this.

"You might have created a monster," I told Suzanne.

The waitress brought my lemonade.

"I am not a monster!" Olive said. She brought a hand to her chest. And then she winked at me before looking around to see if anyone was watching and just popped out.

I heard a gasp behind me. Olive had to have seen that person watching. She just did it for the attention.

"It was a good mystery," Suzanne said. "Don't tell, but

I'm surprised at what a good writer she is. She really missed her calling when she was alive."

"Olive loved working at the hotel," I said. "I think that's why she's still around."

"Fortunately for her, Floyd didn't love this place enough to stick around."

"I'm not sure I could have stayed if he had." I ate another chip. They were good. Nicely salty, slightly spicy, and covered in all sorts of cheeses, beans, and slivers of grilled chicken.

Suzanne nodded. "As much as I enjoyed working on the book with her, I'm sort of glad it's done. I just need to format it and then publish it to the markets and see what happens."

"Cheers," I said lifting my glass. She clinked hers to mine.

It felt good to be sitting back in the hotel sharing food with a friend. I didn't need to go running all over the place finding settings for Olive. She'd have to make do without my help.

About Bonnie Elizabeth

Bonnie Elizabeth could never decide what to do, so she wrote stories about amazing things and sometimes she even finished them.

While rejection stung her so badly in person, she spent most of her young life talking to cats and dogs rather than people, she was unusually resilient when it came to rejections on her writing, racking up a good number of them.

Floating through a variety of jobs, including veterinary receptionist, cemetery administrator, and finally acupuncturist, she continued to write stories.

When the internet came along (yes she's old), she started blogging as her cat, because we all know cats don't notice rejection. Then she started publishing.

Bonnie writes in a variety of genres. Her popular Whisper series is contemporary fantasy and her Teenage Fairy Godmother series is written for teens. She has been published in a number of anthologies and is working on expanding her writing repertoire.

She lives with her husband (who talks less than she does) and her three cats, who always talk back.

Stay in Touch

Also by Bonnie Elizabeth

Familiar Cafe Series

Unfamiliar Magic

Unfair Magic

The Ash Jericho Series

An Inheritance to Die For

A Discovery to Die For

A Distraction to Die For

The Frost Witch Saga

October Snow

November Frost

December Storm

Appalachian Souls

Souls Lost

Souls Broken

The Whisper Novels

Whisper Bound

Taken by the Sound

An Air of Suspicion

Little Dog Lost

Death Interrupted

Down in Whisper

A Haunting Whisper

A Haunting Attraction

Secrets Not Whispers

Only Human

Other Novels

One Bad Wish

Sun Spot Magic

Ghosts from the Past

Unnatural Secrets

Shadows of Solstice

The Haunting of Steely Woods

Find them all at your favorite bookseller or check us out at
MyBigFatOrangeCat.com